Monkey
and Me

Monkey
and Me

DAVID GILMAN

templar

A TEMPLAR BOOK

First published in the UK in 2014
by Templar Publishing,
an imprint of The Templar Company Limited,
Deepdene Lodge, Deepdene Avenue,
Dorking, Surrey, RH5 4AT, UK

Reprinted 2015

www.templarco.co.uk

Text copyright © 2014 David Gilman
Cover illustration by Sarah Horne
Cover design by Will Steele

First UK edition

ISBN 978-1-84877-335-6

This book is for
Denise Ann Gibson

And all the sick kids who have to be braver
than the rest of us.

1

If you look at something, say a telephone pole, or a house, or even a dog sitting in the drive, and you close one eye, whatever you're looking at is in a different place from when you had the other eye closed. That's called perspective. If you close both eyes then you don't see anything and that's called stupid. But if, after rapidly opening and closing each eye, the object jumps left and right, and you're doing this to Mr Peacock's dog-from-hell who's no longer sitting in the drive and is coming at you full tilt because, as everyone knows, staring at a dog is a direct challenge – then that's called suicidal.

"Jez! RUN!" yelled Mark.

He's my brother, and he had a different perspective. He was on the other side of the mesh fence on his way with his mates to try and finish off the last few remaining windows at the derelict Sweet Dreams Sweet Factory. It's a place that made beds called Sweet Dreams, but they closed when the owner went to Thailand on holiday. I think he became what's known as a Missing Person, because the police are still looking for him. Then someone bought it and added the words Sweet Factory. Which was a clever play on words because I often dream of being locked in the school shop and never having to pay for another Swizzle Lick, Juice Fruit Chew or my favourite, Tube Suck. But then they moved their business to China and lots of people around here lost their jobs, including Mum. She was on the Tube Suck quality control line, which is why I got lots of them. She said they were rejects, but that was only because some of the lettering on the packet hadn't come out properly, like Tub Suck or Tube Su k. It still tasted the same.

"Jez! Come on! FASTER!" everyone was shouting.

The dog-from-hell was called Feather but she had a personality disorder and I think that was Mr Peacock's idea of a joke, another play on words. Peacock's Feather. I didn't think it was that clever or even funny; I just thought it was stupid. But I suppose it depends on your perspective.

Mark threw an empty dustbin – the old kind

that Mum used to have before someone in Germany invented the wheelie bin and convinced every government in the world that we all had to have one, at least that's what Dad says – as Skimp hauled me through the torn fence, which saved me from being savaged to death. And he also did Feather a favour, because the Dangerous Dogs Act would have meant that Feather would have been put to sleep. Not that she had ever, ever bitten anyone; she just liked to scare all the kids in the street. But you never know – one day she might get the taste for human flesh and then the street population of children would be shredded. Bits and pieces of bones and entrails would lead armed police to her lair next to Mr Peacock's compost bin and then…

"That was really dumb. You know you can't mess about with that fleabag!" Mark shouted at me as I sat trying to get my breath back. Big wheezing gulps that made my chest feel as though it had sandpaper inside.

"You can't come with us if you can't keep up!" Skimp said, though I know he didn't mean it.

"And stopping and doing things like opening and closing one eye," said Pete-the-Feet.

"It's called perspective," I told him.

"This gang has to be light on its feet. We have to move like a Rapid Deployment Force, responding to every danger without hesitation. Not standing around picking your nose while Peacock's Paranoid Pet attacks," Rocky said.

I tried to imagine standing with my finger up my nose as Peacock's Feather attacked. But I couldn't. Bogey picking would seriously slow down your escape.

Mark's gang always let me go along with them although I wasn't in double digits. You had to be ten or older to join and I was nine years, eleven months and seven days, so I was designated Probationary Gang Member, though Rocky said I was Tail-end Charlie. This was what anyone at the back of an army patrol was called and, as I was always bringing up the rear, it sort of made sense, even though we weren't actually in the army like Rocky's uncle.

Gangs, I discovered, are not democratic. Pete-the-Feet, Skimp and Rocky had voted against me joining, but after Mark had called an Extraordinary Meeting of the Executive Council, and took them to one side, they all came back and voted me in.

After all, it's his gang and I'm his brother, so it's always good to have a relative in a position of power. That's called nepotism.

Anyway, we broke four windows on the third floor, with the best throw going to Pete-the-Feet, who took a run at the corner of the building, threw the half brick like Freddie Flintoff on a fast wicket and bowled out the fourth floor corner window. He was going so fast he fell head over heels and tore the back of his jacket, which we thought was hilarious, but his mum would give him what-for because she paid seven pounds fifty for it at the Oxfam shop.

All in all it was a lot of fun. No one got eaten alive and we got our own back on the man who took away our sweets and Mum's job. Somewhere in an unpronounceable province of China I bet there's another boy getting reject Tube Sucks because his mum says the letter is missing. I wonder what a missing 'c' or 'e' is in their alphabet. Maybe I should learn Chinese, then I could always emigrate to the unpronounceable province, move in with the boy's family, teach him English and share his reject Tube Sucks. I'll ask Dad and see if he can't get transferred to the Chinese Post Office. Life should be an adventure, that's what he always says, and you can't get a bigger adventure than becoming a Chinese postman.

Because I get tired after an exhausting day breaking windows (well, half an hour probably) I always like going home. I think it's the toast, though Mum and Dad are also part of it. But toast always fills the house with a smell that makes my mouth water. Mark says it's a Pavlovian response – I thought that was some kind of foreign cake he was talking about. Hot toast – home – mouth-watering – hug from Mum. It's learned behaviour, says my know-it-all brother, which I think is a bit rich coming from him, because he never seems to learn things except the hard way. He's always getting thumped by Ronnie Rogers, who's bigger than him. How many times have I told him –"Don't pick fights with kids who are bigger and better fighters than you are." But every week, sometimes once a day, there he is whacking Rogers with his schoolbag and wrestling him to the ground. I don't know why he does it, and he won't tell me either. I think Mark's a bit too sensitive for his age, that's what Mum says too, while Dad just puts his arm around him and speaks quietly to him out in the garden, then they kick a ball around for a while. Being sensitive is difficult for a twelve-year-old boy. I'm sensitive as well, but I'm only nine years, eleven months and seven days old and that must make a difference, I suppose. Besides, I've learned to ignore what Gobby Rogers and his mates yell at me. I like the way I look. I've got no choice. I wear a beanie hat all the time and that's what everyone calls me – Beanie. That's what's called a nickname but it can also be an insult – it's all about perspective again. I think it's a great beanie. It's got a nice soft cotton lining and a red, black and orange knit that makes my head look like a wasp. It keeps my head and ears warm and it muffles the insults. It's perfect. And I wear it everywhere, I mean all the time, even in the bath, except when Mum whips it off and lathers my head with soap that smells like…

"Mark! Look at this scratch on Jez's neck."

"It's nothing, Mum," I told her as I got the toast and raspberry jam in as far as it would go.

"Don't talk with your mouth full, Jez. How many times do I have to tell you?"

"But you're always telling me to eat while the food's hot. If I waited it'd be cold."

"Don't be clever, it doesn't suit you." Which shows how grown-ups always contradict themselves. Mum's usually telling me how clever I am.

"He got caught going under a fence, that's all," Mark explained.

"And if Skimp hadn't pulled me through, Peacock's Feather would've…" A swift kick to the shins under the table nearly made me choke and I regurgitated a clump of soggy bread and jam. It was disgusting, but it took Mum's mind off asking any more questions. She fussed and patted my back, wiped my face and slumped in the chair between us.

She seemed a bit tired today. I wondered if it was the visits to the hospital. Mum and Dad are beginning to cause me some concern. She's a bit weepy and Dad often puts his arms around her, not at the same time as Mark, but you have to think that his arms are put to a lot of use in our house. Mark knows something, but isn't saying. I wonder if she's pregnant. She's getting a bit old for another baby and she'd never manage because she's always saying Mark and me are a handful. Though, to be fair, she doesn't say that as much any more.

She sipped her tea. "Mark, don't let Jez get hurt, all right? You promised."

He nodded and pinched the last piece of toast.

I didn't know he'd promised. It's most likely because he's older and it's the burden of responsibility that big brothers have. I suppose if she is pregnant then I'll have to do the same for the new baby. Anyway, that's something I can't even think about because by the time it goes to school I'll be too old. They'll have to hire a private bodyguard instead.

Mum smiled at me. "Come on, let's get some antiseptic on that scratch. We don't want it getting infected."

Anyone would think the Sweet Dreams Sweet Factory's fence had been contaminated with bubonic plague to keep kids out. What if it hadn't been a sweet factory? What if they used that as cover for a secret biological warfare plant? Maybe they've sold deadly germs to the Chinese instead of Tube Sucks and Swizzle Licks. The words undercover and subterfuge sprang to mind – deception and spying. Vital information that puts everyone's life in danger. Maybe Mum had inside information. Maybe she was part of a Witness Protection Programme, which was why she's on Checkout 14 at Sainsbury's. It was a secret identity.

"Mum, were those Tube Sucks really what you said they were?"

"What?"

"Were the missing letters on the label really some kind of code? Was quality control some kind of weapons' grade inspection facility? How could the government let the Chinese have our secrets for germ warfare? Were you really on subterfuge duty?"

By now we'd reached the bathroom, and she was looking for the tube of antiseptic. "Subterfuge? How do you know words like that? Where do you get all these ideas from?"

"*Everything You Need to Know in the World.* Volume Five. Seventy-five p at the RSPCA charity shop."

She shook her head and squeezed the ointment. "This is the closest I'll ever get to germ warfare. Keep still."

That wasn't a definite no, then.

2

You know how sometimes you wake up in the morning and you don't know where you are? That happens to me quite a lot. I lie still and there's just me and the duvet in some kind of cloud formation floating in a Nowhere Zone. I can't hear anything. I'm not asleep but I'm not really awake either, so I drift along like a feather being bumped by the breeze. Then I know what it is I'm remembering. Dad's cab. There are 308,562 kilometres of roads in the UK, give or take the odd country lane, and Dad used to drive a monster articulated lorry everywhere there was a road big enough to drive down. All in all, with the trailer, it was an eighteen-wheeler, 13.6 metres long, three axles and six super singles; that's what you call the wheels because there's six of them and they're all singles. And the nice thing about the Scania Topliner was that it had two bunks behind the cab. The one above the driver's seat was for me.

That's where I used to snuggle when we went on those long journeys during school holidays and where Dad hid me when we went into the docks to unload, because it's illegal to take kids there – so I'd stay wedged behind the curtain. There was a fridge, microwave and a telly, it was heated, and if I'm honest I preferred being in there to being in my own room. I think with a bit more time I could have driven it myself, though the sixteen gears might have taken a bit of getting used to. I've eaten Dundee cake in Dundee and scones and cream in Devon, and I've scoffed fish and chips in Whitby, but didn't fancy the jellied eels in east London. That's called discretion. Or, as Mark says, that's me being chicken. But I don't eat chicken any more either since I saw on the telly how thousands of them are crammed into sheds. That's horrible. That's cheap food, says Mark. That's like a concentration camp, Dad says and Mum now has to buy cowboy chickens, which is what Dad calls them because they are free-range. I still don't eat them. So, that's the feeling I have lying under my duvet – rocking gently along, to the purring of Dad's big diesel engine, swaying me gently beneath the duvet in the sleeping cab behind him.

But I don't go with him any more. He gave up being a long-distance lorry driver because he said he wanted to be closer to home, what with Mum working shifts at the supermarket and everything. I miss the cab, but I'm glad he's home. So's Mum. I think it's the hospital thing again.

Sometimes, on my way home, I watch him (when he's on a double round) pushing that big trolley with the huge red Royal Mail bag strapped to it. He's not that young any more and I wish I could think of something to get him back on the road with McKinley's Transport Company Limited, so he could sit in his nice heated cab with the pneumatic seat, his power steering and the comfy bunk in the back of the cab with the little telly set up. Maybe I could get Mark's gang to steal his postman's trolley, then he'd get sacked. But losing the Royal Mail is a pretty serious offence, and how cross would the Queen be if all the postcards of Windsor Castle she sent everyone never got delivered? It might be better to sneak out at night and seal up all the letter boxes, then he couldn't deliver any mail. If I wrote to everyone I know I could ask them never to write to anyone ever again, that might make his load lighter;

but the trouble with that idea is that he would have to deliver the letters that I've written. I'll have to think about this again.

My brain often jumbles loads of thoughts together. I can hear Feather barking down the street and Mrs Tomkinson shouting, "Shut that flaming dog up!" Light creeps around and through the curtains (they're not very thick: X-Men prints, seventy per cent cotton, thirty per cent poly-something – the label's worn away – made in China).

Mum's shouting for Mark and me to get up. In the half-light I see Steven Gerrard's poster on the wall, leg extended, striking the ball. Michael Owen (who was arguably the world's best ever player for Liverpool – before Steven Gerrard, that is) doesn't play for Liverpool any more. Even though he left home, and went to play for another club – whose name shall not be mentioned (says Dad) – he's still here, in our hearts (says Dad). He never really went away. You don't. It's where you belong. That's called Emotional Ties.

Then I have to pee.

This was a capital letter day. It was a BIG day.

When countries declare war they have special meetings in the War Room. Skimp and Rocky were sitting on the wall during break. Mark was kicking his ball, concentrating hard, though not on the kicking – he just does that on automatic – but on what Skimp had just told him.

"It's being pulled down."

"What is?" I asked.

"Clear off, Jez," Mark said, "this is an EMEC – an Extraordinary Meeting of the Executive Council."

"About what?"

"They're demolishing Sweet Dreams," said Pete-the-Feet.

"Shut up, you! EMECs are secret!" Mark hit him on the head with the ball.

"Well, it's not a secret now," Rocky said, retrieving it.

"Beanie's on the council anyway," Skimp told them. "He's already been voted into the gang, so how can we keep him out?"

They all looked at Mark and he looked at me. He must have realised that the process of democratic decision-making sometimes overrules nepotism.

"All right. Look, we've got to find a new

headquarters," Mark told us. I could see he was back in command again.

"Why can't we keep the factory?" I asked.

They look at me as if I was deaf, like that Tracy Lewis who lives across the other side of the estate and goes to a special school. "I mean, they can't knock it down all at once. There must be a bit of it we can use."

"You're not allowed to make suggestions, Beanie. You're still on probation," Rocky said. "Besides, we could get trapped underground and end up like Hitler in his bunker."

I didn't think Hitler was ever at the Sweet Dreams Sweet Factory, but I didn't say anything.

"We could always have a protest," Pete-the-Feet suggested. "Y'know, link arms, 'We shall not be moved,' and all that. I mean, perhaps Sweet Dreams might even be some kind of Victorian heritage building. We could tell everyone it's important to the nation."

"After we've smashed all the windows, I don't think so," said Skimp.

"There's one window left," I told them. "The fourth floor, top right."

"So what? There won't be any floors left after today," Rocky moaned.

Then the bell went. Obviously we were in some kind of crisis. The gang's secret hideout was about to be demolished. "Dad says we must never give up without a fight," I shouted at them as they walked back.

"You can't fight bulldozers, Beanie. Get real," Rocky said.

I stood there watching everyone go back into school. You can't get real. It's not something you can touch or smell. It's something else. It's called a figure of speech. But being real is different – that's being yourself. At least that's what Dad says. And I know who I am. I'm Jez Matthews, I'm nine years, eleven months and eight days old.

And, as Dad keeps telling me, if you don't try, you don't get. He never finishes that sentence – but I think I know what he means. You can't give up without a fight.

It was sports afternoon, and circumstances meant I was excused. 'Circumstances' is a word I never knew much about – I didn't have to because I never really had any. Circumstances, that is. But now I hear it a lot. Dad gave up his lorry-driving because of circumstances, Mum works shifts at the supermarket because of circumstances and I don't play football because of circumstances. Thirteen is an unlucky number and there are thirteen letters in that word – and it seems to me that circumstances are never really that good. So on sports day my circumstances allow me to run home and sneak into Dad's shed.

He's brilliant at everything. He was a very careful long-distance lorry driver and he's a well-liked postie who keeps an eye on elderly people when he delivers mail. He might be brilliant at everything he does, but no one's told him that he's not so brilliant at DIY. In fact he's rubbish, that's the truth. When he tried to decorate the house last year we had more wallpaper left over than the Dead Sea Scrolls, or so Mum said.

And another thing: Dad never throws anything out. You never know when you might need something again, he always tells Mum. Then she insists he puts whatever it is in the shed. Where no one goes except him. And me.

I had to tell the world about Sweet Dreams Sweet

Factory and thanks to Dad's hoarding and all those rolls of wallpaper I had everything I needed. I was going to make a banner big enough to be seen from space, though I doubted that anyone up there in the international space station would be looking down just at the right time.

It took me a while to saw the broom handle in half with Dad's small handsaw and then tack each end of the wallpaper roll onto the two halves. Then I needed a long corridor to unroll my banner. And Dad's shed isn't even big enough to swing a cat in – or so he says – so I took it in the house and unrolled it in the hall. I got marker pen ink on me, the walls and Mum's beige carpet. She wouldn't be pleased if she noticed, and it would be hard to miss because where I'd gone over the edge of the paper looked like crows' feet had walked in ink and staggered up the hall. But once she knew I'd done exactly what Dad had always told me, then I doubted that she'd throw a wobbly.

He's always said we have to be brave. I don't know why, because we don't have rampaging elephants coming down the street, there are no cobras in the garden and the nearest motorway is miles away.

As long as you can outrun Peacock's Feather there's nothing really to worry about around here. I think maybe he meant school and the other kids. But I'm not sure. He never said. And when I asked him why I had to be brave he didn't seem too sure, but then said we shouldn't be scared.

I didn't know I was.

So, everything was going to plan until I got to the top floor of Sweet Dreams Sweet Factory. Some of the big earth-moving machines were at the back of the building and there was brick dust everywhere. Every time one of the JCBs whacked the building with its mutant-crab-like arm, the whole place shuddered. The stairwells were still okay and luckily the breeze came through all those windows we'd broken and blew fresh air inside, which stopped the dust from choking me. I think my timing was a bit out. I didn't think my protest was going to save the building.

I got to the edge and climbed out onto the old fire-escape. Then I unfurled the wallpaper roll for the whole world to see. It dangled like a banner from a high-street shop when they have a sale, but my banner didn't say 'Everything Must Go 50%

Off'; mine said 'SAVE SWEET DREAMS SWEET FACTOR'.

Sometimes when I write an essay I run out of space on the edge of the page and I have to break the word up and carry on the next line. Well, I ran out of space with my banner. I couldn't fit the Y in. But I didn't have another line to go on. So people are either going to think I can't spell or won't know what Factor it is we should be trying to save. Some might be bright enough to know I ran out of paper.

I waited an hour but no one turned up to see my protest and it'd gone very quiet. I thought the demolition men had gone home. And the fire escape felt wonky. It creaked and groaned and I noticed it was quite rusty. I thought I might be too heavy for such an old bit of iron. My banner was flapping a bit as the wind picked up and I tried to climb back into the building. But as I put my feet on the railing it came away from the wall. Not much. But enough. It was a gap big enough to fit my lunch box in, between the wall and railing. I got this sudden lurch in my stomach and I caught my breath, because if it came away from the wall any more I was going to have a problem. Like falling.

I must have been really clumsy and left too many clues at home, because I saw Mark and Dad arrive in the car and Mark was already pointing up.

"Jez! Stay there, son! Don't move!" Dad shouted.

I waved, but the iron fire escape wobbled. I held on and had to grip the railing tighter because my knees were trembling and all of a sudden it seemed a long way down to where Mark stood alone looking up at me.

"You idiot! You absolute moron!" he shouted by way of making me feel better and to disguise his true feelings of concern for me.

Then, all of a sudden, there was a crowd of people and kids, standing on the other side of the fence. Maybe they'd come to offer their support to save the factory. And right over there, coming down Jessup Road, was a police car with its lights flashing. I'm not so sure they were there for crowd control.

Then I went all wobbly. That's happened before once in a while, but just then was not a good time to faint. I gripped the old iron tighter. My nose was running, but I couldn't let go to wipe it. Then I found it was bleeding. Dad calls it a Bloody Nuisance Nose – it happens now and again.

Then I saw Dad. He popped his head through a broken window. He smiled and rolled his eyes. He always sees the funny side of things. Dad's a lot of fun. Sometimes when we're all out together he embarrasses Mum. There we are walking down the shopping mall and suddenly he jumps in front of us, opens up his big hands and stops us dead in our tracks.

We know what's coming.

"Jim! Don't!" Mum warns him.

But he puts on his mad face which cracks us up. Then he starts. "What do we want?"

And Mark and I shout back: "Each other!"

"And when do we want it?" he yells.

"Now!"

And we all give high fives. And then he does it again because Mum looks fit to die but he won't stop until she joins in.

"What do we want?"

"Each other!" we shout back and even Mum joins in – she has to or he'll keep on doing this until someone calls security.

"When do we want it?"

"NOW!"

Then Mum's also laughing.

"You're certifiable, you are, Jim Matthews," she tells him.

"Well, I'd have to be, coming to the shops on a Saturday with you lot."

It's just one of those moments. It's called magic.

I think being stuck up there on an old fire escape that was about to fall four stories into broken rubble might have been what Dad meant about being scared. What he never mentioned was the embarrassment of being rescued. I was never really frightened, but it was extremely embarrassing. Dad reached down and grabbed me and put me over his shoulder – like a sack of coal. And when we got down to the ground there was an even bigger crowd. I closed my eyes tight. That was the only way I could stop everyone gawping. The police said something about trespassing, Dad told them I was only a lad and they said something about at least no one was hurt. Dad was agreeing and said that he'd take me home.

I didn't listen to the funny remarks and laughter from the crowd. If you close your eyes tight enough it can affect your hearing.

I think that's called turning a blind ear.

Of course they took me to the hospital – because of the nose bleed – and this set Mum off because of the whole smelly antiseptic hospital thing. I think she just got scared. And I got fussed over and everyone clucked and cooed like I was a chicken or a pigeon who'd hurt itself climbing out the nest. There was nothing wrong with me but Mum and Dad hovered outside the examination area whispering to the doctor. People whisper in hospitals with doctors because it's impolite and embarrassing to let everyone know what's wrong with you. Dad did his arm-hugging thing with Mum and that seemed to calm her down.

You know how it is when things frighten you and someone hugs you and says, "There there, it'll be all right pet," or "chuck," or "sweetheart…" they might even use your name once in a while… well, that's how it was with Mum.

Anyway, Mum took the rest of the day off to stay home with me. There would be a lot of unhappy customers at Sainsbury's. Checkout 14 is very popular.

I'd been sick before I went to bed. I think it was the

double-thick chocolate sponge pudding with custard
that did it (Mum gets a discount) but Mark scoffed
more than me and he was all right. But as I drifted
off to sleep I was busy scoring the winning goal for
Liverpool against Chelsea. Steven Gerrard passed
a long curving ball, Gobby Rogers was defending
for Chelsea – how did he make the team? – and he
was coming at me like a National Express coach on
the M6. I could hear the crowd roaring, "Beanie,
Beanie, BEANIE!" It was a wave of sound and I
was riding it like the Silver Surfer. Gobby Rogers
snarled, like he always does, and as I jigged left, he
stuck his foot out – that would be a foul and we'd get
the penalty. Typical Rogers. Can't think further than
the end of his foot. I didn't want a penalty. I wasn't
going to take a dive. I tapped the ball with my ankle,
it bounced over him and I followed it. Rogers was
sliding away into touch and there were no red shirts
in the box, only Mr Forsyth, our Head Teacher who
for some reason was playing goalie and looked more
agile than I'd ever seen him. There were no strikers
anywhere. Chelsea players swarmed at me. "Beanie!
Beanie!" The crowd roared. It was deafening. I don't
know how I did it but I got through the defenders.

It went quiet. Everything slowed down. Just me and Mr Forsyth, who never took his eyes off the ball as he crouched in defence. For some reason I noticed he'd got really knobbly knees.

The muscles in my leg tightened, I balanced my weight with my arms, head over the ball – I mentally thanked Steven Gerrard for showing me how to strike the ball like this. But I couldn't kick it. Something was holding my leg. Mark's voice came from the other side of the penalty area. He thought he had a clear shot. He didn't. But he kept yelling at me. "Jez! Jez! Come on!"

With superhuman effort I kicked the ball. It started off low, gained height and then the fade I'd put into the strike made it curve, ever so slowly, above Mr Forsyth's outstretched hands. He couldn't get to it. The glare of the lights blinded me for a few seconds, the faces in the crowd froze, and the ball dropped behind him. It had to be a goal, it had to be...

"JEZ!"

Someone's switched the floodlights off.

Mark was tugging at my foot. "Wake up," he whispered. "Come on."

He pulled me out of bed and I followed him to the window. Maybe I was still asleep. I could hear the crowd still singing the Liverpool FC anthem:

"When you walk through a storm,
Hold your head up high,
And don't be afraid of the dark.
At the end of the storm,
There's a golden sky,
And the sweet silver song of a lark…"

But now it sounded like there was only one voice.

Mark pulled the curtain back a bit and put a finger to his lips. We looked down into the back garden. Dad had a can of beer in his hand, and he was singing to the moon, except there wasn't one. It was raining. Mum always tells us not to hang about in the rain. You can get cold, and that can lead to bronchitis and then pneumonia and then…

"What's he doing? There wasn't a match tonight," I whispered to Mark.

"Shush," was all he said.

"Walk on, walk on, with hope in your heart… and you'll never walk alone… you'll… never… walk alone…"

Dad slumped onto the grass. Mum always says

you get piles if you sit on wet ground. Then we heard Mrs Tomkinson shout, "Shut that flaming racket up!"

He threw his beer can over the garden fence. It wasn't very aggressive, because Dad isn't.

"He's had a few," Mark says quietly. I looked at him. He looked worried. We'd never seen Dad like this before.

Then Mum came out. "Oh, Jim. Come on, love, come on."

Dad looked really sad. I thought he'd got rain in his eyes. She sat and put her arms around him. "Don't… it's all right, love. It'll be all right."

She hugged him like she hugs us but this was different. Then she gave him a little kiss on his head and held him to her. Like he was a little boy. They both sat in the rain holding each other.

I think Dad misses Michael Owen.

And he knows he's never coming back.

3

In a way I'm relieved that the Sweet Dreams Sweet Factory wasn't a secret germ warfare establishment because I'd probably have bubonic plague by now and that would mean going into hospital again and I've been there a lot – and that would upset Mum even more. I am disappointed that she isn't any kind of secret agent, though she questioned me like I was a spy. Why was I out there? Why was I trying to save the building? What did I think I was doing? Didn't I know I could get hurt doing that sort of thing? Didn't I think she had enough to worry about?

She was really upset and kept going on and on, and when she has one of those turns the best thing to do is to just keep quiet. Besides, she asked all those questions without even taking a breath, so I couldn't have said anything anyway. Though in fairness she never mentioned the stains on the carpet. Mark sat across the table with his eyes screwed up, glaring at me, waiting for me to crack under the pressure and tell everyone that the Sweet Dreams Sweet Factory, soon to provide housing for hundreds of new kids who will start gangs of their own, was our secret headquarters. But I didn't crack.

You'd have thought that would make me a full gang member, resisting interrogation like that, especially as Mum had tears in her eyes. Skimp and Rocky thought I was awesome, so I didn't tell them I was really quite scared, there's no point in destroying people's illusions. That's called bursting their bubble.

Mark doesn't have a bubble.

"You were irresponsible!" he yelled. "If you'd have fallen and got mangled in all the metal then it would have made headlines in the local paper – *Mashed-up Boy was Secret Gang Member*. And then the whole gang would have been dragged into it and we'd all be grounded for ever because parents always think the worst when they hear the word 'gang'."

I could sense another vote coming on. And even though Skimp and Rocky thought I was one step away from joining the X-Men, Mark could convince them to take away my probationary status.

"Beanie did all right," Rocky said. But I could

tell he was just being nice in front of me – after all, he is the gang's 2IC and second-in-command has to carry some burden of responsibility.

"He was striking a note for freedom," Skimp added.

"No, he wasn't," said Mark, pointing a finger at me while he looked aggressively at Skimp. "He was trying to be a martyr. That's what he always does. He's always the centre of attention."

That was news to me. I thought martyrs were burned at the stake and that Simon Cowell was the centre of attention in our house, though Mum says he should be burned at the stake. I didn't see any connection with any of that and my protest at Sweet Dreams. Maybe if I'd fallen and got impaled on the old iron railings that would have made me a martyr and everyone would have rallied around and saved the old place. Then it occurred to me, out of nowhere, just a burst of light in my head, that Mark, who got new trainers for his birthday, had really wanted my Number 8 shirt.

"You can have my shirt if you want."

"What?"

"I said…"

"Put your coat back on! Mum'll kill me if you catch cold. I don't want your stupid shirt. That's got nothing to do with anything."

"I'll have it, Beanie," Rocky said.

"No, you won't!" Mark said, stepping between us. "Our dad got him that and it cost an arm and a leg. Jez! Put-your-coat-on! Do as you're told."

For some reason everyone was upset that day.

"I was only trying to save our headquarters," I told him. "I thought that if I did that I could be a fully paid-up member of the gang."

Skimp and Rocky looked away as if they didn't know what to say. Skimp opened his mouth but Mark glared at him – and Skimp closed it again. Maybe he was just yawning. Hanging about for hours on end can be pretty tiring.

Mark looked at me. "I'm sorry, Jez, you'd better go home. I can't risk you doing another stupid stunt and getting hurt. Mum and Dad would give me too much grief," he said, putting his hand on my shoulder, like he was saying goodbye for ever. "And besides you can't keep up."

"I'll try harder." I was getting a horrible feeling in my stomach. I think it's called desperation.

I didn't want to be left out of the gang.

"He could go up front," Rocky suggested. "That's what they do on army patrols. Slowest man sets the pace."

Mark might be my brother but I think Skimp and Rocky are the only friends I have, and Pete-the-Feet, of course, who was running like a greyhound after a rabbit. He's like that. Ultra. Greased lightning, though in truth lightning can't be greased, that's fairly obvious, it would never be able to stay up there and grip the clouds, would it? We'd have lightning falling out the sky like icicles all the time.

Pete-the-Feet can run faster and further than anyone we know. He started training when he was very young, running away from his stepdad, who used him as a punchbag. And Pete-the-Feet is so tall and skinny one good thump could shatter him like glass. Best to run when you can.

"I've got it!" he gulped after a big spit to clear his lungs. He looked as though he'd run a marathon.

My mind spun for a moment. Was he a plague carrier? Is that what he'd got?

Everyone watched him. He had a mad look in his eye, not that that's too unusual. Sometimes after he's been running his hair smothers his face and gets stuck with sweat so he looks a bit like the Abominable Snowman and all you can see are these two black eyes peering out – like a scared creature peering through bushes. I think Pete-the-Feet hides in there when it suits him. His feet help him escape, his hair is his secret den.

Then he uttered the words that could scare anyone to death. "The Black Gate."

Mark miskicked the ball. I've never seen him do that before. It caught Rocky on the side of the head and for a minute I thought he was going to thump Mark. Rocky can be a bit aggressive at times.

"You're off your head!" Skimp said.

"Nobody goes in there!" Rocky told him.

"I know. That's the beauty of it. No one will know where we are. It's the perfect HQ. We don't have to actually go into the house, there's a few old ruined buildings in the grounds."

The Black Gate. You might as well suggest we dig up a grave in the cemetery and climb in the hole with the dead, even that wouldn't be as scary as going into the Black Gate.

Pete-the-Feet can run fast but his brain tends

to lag behind a bit. A bit like a relay race.

"Just under the fence. That's all we have to do. There's a least half a dozen acres and we don't have to go anywhere near the house," he gabbled.

Everybody knows that there are creatures in there that can sneak out the grass, fall out a tree, jump out the dark, snatch you from the bushes, and then drag you screaming into the Black Gate – which is what the old country house is called. It was a couple of miles beyond where all the other houses had been built. It had been sold off years ago but there was some kind of legal stuff that stopped anyone buying it and redeveloping the site. There's a huge sign over the old iron gates: *Dangerous Building – Condemned – Keep Out.* Along the top of the old walls are strands of barbed wire to make sure no one can get in, but you wouldn't want to because everyone knows there's something inhuman in the Black Gate. People have heard screams and sounds of someone moving round inside, but when the police investigated they didn't find anyone – or anything.

Definitely haunted then.

And obviously by a creature with fangs and claws – a throwback mutation that could have been created when the sewage works blocked up last year and spilled into Millbrook's Farm. It flooded five acres of King Edward potatoes with disgusting stuff which stank for months – but it gave the farmer a bumper crop. I've never eaten spuds since then. Not even Mum's beyond excellent thick-cut home-made chips. Can you imagine what she'd be deep-fat frying? Sealing in all the goodness, she used to say. I don't think so, Mum.

"You're off your head," Skimp said again.

"Well, we could always leg it if it got too scary," Pete-the-Feet replied.

He would say that, wouldn't he?

"What? And leave us for bait?" Rocky pointed a finger at him.

"No one's ever got out of there alive," I told them.

"Don't talk rubbish, Beanie," Rocky said.

"No one's ever died in there," said Mark.

"That's because no one knows how many people have gone in and never come out," I tell them.

I'm not sure even Pete-the-Feet could run fast enough to escape the ghosts and sabre-toothed monsters, whose teeth are probably all gunged up with the remains of anything that walked or crawled in there. Kimberley Morris says her brother went in and hasn't been heard of since – but everyone knows he really got nicked for stealing cars and is in prison. Still… you never know. She and her mum and dad have never visited him. So maybe he's not – in prison I mean. Or alive.

I hear myself say words that make no sense to my brain… I don't know where I get these ideas from sometimes. Like climbing up onto the Sweet Dreams Sweet Factory top floor, or the time I tried to balance across the old stone bridge and fell in the canal, or when I climbed the tree and the branch gave way and I broke my wrist – and that started a lot of problems. Hospitals! But even they aren't as frightening as the Black Gate. You'd have to be two spanners short of a tool set to even think about going in there… but the words fell out my mouth. It was so cold all the letters froze in the air and you could have hung them on a clothes line.

"I'll go inside. I'll do it. I will. You'll see."

"You're going home," said Mark. "It was a mistake letting you join the gang."

"He's only a probationary member," Skimp reminded him.

A gang member is a gang member even if he is a probationary. That's called semantics. I'd have mentioned this, but Mark would say I was just being a know-it-all clever-clogs.

Rocky had a strange look on his face. I've seen him like that when we go round his house – he's got a great collection of war and horror movies which we're not supposed to watch. It's a bit like him drooling in front of a sweet shop. There's something very needy about Rocky.

"Let him do it," he said.

"No way!" said Mark. "I'm not getting grounded for the rest of my life because Jez gets devoured by some creature from a hidden tomb in Black Gate's cellars."

"I want to do it! And you can't stop me." There were all those words dangling in front of my face again. Where did they come from? But I had to show Mark and the others that I didn't need looking after all the time.

Skimp nodded. "I think Rocky is right. Beanie should go in if that's what he wants. Then, if he doesn't come out, we'll know it's true about the monster. But if he does come out alive then everyone will stop picking on him because we'll be witnesses that he dared to go in."

Suddenly Mark was wrestling Skimp to the ground. "He's my brother! He doesn't have to prove anything!"

Rocky and Pete-the-Feet pulled him off.

"Yes, I do," I said. "I'm not scared." And this time the air from my breath held the words like angels dancing on a cloud.

It must have been cold because everyone froze in that moment. They all looked at me. And then Rocky broke the silence. "Me neither."

"Nor me." Skimp.

"All right. Let's do it." Pete-the-Feet.

We all looked at Mark. This was a command decision. His whole future as a possible world leader was in the balance.

"We'll go in as far as we can," Mark said.

"And Beanie?" Rocky asked. "He should go in first. It was his idea."

"He stays behind me."

And the way Mark said it everyone knew there wasn't going to be any argument.

4

Being scared is blaming the cold when you shiver. But when your legs are trembling so much that you couldn't run away if you had to, that's like living in an igloo with no clothes on.

"It's getting really cold," I said.

They looked at me and nodded because they were shivering too. Skimp hugged himself, maybe he was trying to keep from running away by holding himself down. We skirted the walls and found a few slippery handholds, there was moss growing on the one side and Rocky told us that means it's north facing. I didn't know if that was true or not. I didn't care. All I knew was I wouldn't be able to climb the wall there. So we trudged around a bit further. Mark was in front, then me, then Skimp, Pete-the-Feet and Rocky was Tail-end Charlie. And he kept looking over his shoulder.

I noticed we were all whispering. We reached the gates, and they were huge, much bigger than

I remembered them. They were like prison gates with spikes on top. They were rusty in places and the grass and weeds had grown all round the hinges and the bars. We looked up at the sign: *Dangerous Building – Condemned – Keep Out.*

Condemned. That's like being executed or something.

Only Pete-the-Feet was tall enough to see the house's roof in the far distance above the undergrowth.

"There's no sign of life," he said.

And we all looked at him. Of course there was no sign of life – it was haunted!

"You're as daft as a brush, you are," Mark told him.

"We'll never get over these gates," said Mark. And I think there was a bit of relief in his voice.

"We can squeeze through here," Skimp said, and rubbed his hand between the iron gate and the wall. Some of the stone had crumbled and the gap was just choked with weeds.

"Nice one, Skimp," said Pete-the-Feet. But I don't think he meant it as a compliment.

"You said you wanted to find a way in, well, here it is."

"Yeah, but maybe not right now. This is just a recce," Rocky whispered.

Mark looked at his watch. It's supposed to be a Swiss Army watch, but it's just a knockoff we got down the market, so it's not always as accurate as a Swiss watch would be and there are times I hope the real Swiss Army has real Swiss Army watches because if they haven't and they've bought a knockoff like us, they're never going to be on time for anything – like avalanches, which appear to happen at fairly regular intervals. Though I don't think you can time them.

"It's nearly ten past," Mark said, "Mum'll be home soon for our tea."

Rocky looked at his watch. His is an Argos digital. It always works. It was really cheap too, cheaper than Mark's Swiss Army knockoff – it just didn't have the little red cross logo, but so what? He was always on time because he said soldiers had to be in the right place when they were supposed to – that's called getting to the RV. I've never really had an RV – which means rendezvous – unless it's getting out of bed and down to breakfast on time. I don't need a watch for that because Mum always shouts so loud, Dad says she could wake the dead.

The dead.

"Are timeless."

"What?" Mark said.

"The dead are timeless," I told him. "They don't need watches. Ghosts hover everywhere all the time, even in monster form. It depends on the light. When the light fades and it gets darker, they suck it in and that gives them a shape to their bodies."

"What are you on about?" Skimp asked.

"It doesn't matter what time it is, as long as it's daylight. I think we'll be safe as long as we are out of there by the time it's dark."

Skimp checked his watch. "Mine says a quarter to," he said.

"It's exactly eleven minutes to," Rocky said. "If we're going to do this we'd better be quick about it because it might take us ages to get to the house. I think that's an animal track through the bushes."

No one said anything for a minute because we were all thinking of what kind of animal could have made it. One thing was for sure – I knew it wasn't made by the postman. Because that's my dad and he's never been here in his life. I suppose it could be someone getting in to read the electricity meter.

I've heard of people being sent electric bills when they're dead. But I don't think that's the case here. No one in their right mind would really go into the Black Gate.

I squeezed between the gate and the pillar.

Sometimes you just have to be brave. That's what Dad says when we go to the hospital.

It doesn't matter how many times you see a scary movie or read a book about vampires or monsters or graveyards where people pop out the ground and grab you and drag you below – walking in the grounds of a haunted house is a hundred times worse than that. Because he was leader of the gang Mark had to go first and because I was his brother I went second, the others shuffled and shouldered each other because no one really wanted to be Tail-end Charlie. Everyone, but everyone knows the last person in line always get snatched first. It's the law.

Rocky ended up at the back but he found a hefty stick and promised everyone that if anything twitched in the bushes he was going to attack it. But by the time we got to the old gravel driveway that looped around the house like a snake curling around its victim, nothing had moved. We hadn't even heard a bird singing. Things were worse than I thought.

The windows were boarded up and there was no way inside so we edged around the back of the house where huge, stone-edged windows stood like upright soldiers guarding the place with the boards looking like their shields. The terraced gardens were completely overgrown, but below the first terrace was some kind of entrance, which might have been where the gardeners kept all their tools. The old wooden door was rotten and half off its hinges and Pete-the-Feet and Skimp pulled it away carefully and as quietly as they could. It was like a small cave inside, with the old stone walls dribbling with water. There were a few ruined old tools, a rake, a couple of spades and a rotten wooden wheelbarrow. It was like an ancient tomb.

"I bet there's bodies buried down here," Pete-the-Feet said.

It was highly unlikely because we could all see this was a garden store that just happened to be underneath one of the terraces, but still we shoved each other to get outside. I'm not sure if that's called panic or imagination.

By the time we had gone through the gardens and climbed up the other side of the house we saw a padlocked door on the side of the house. The gravel crunched beneath our feet. We stopped and looked at each other. It's very difficult to tiptoe quietly on gravel. Skimp had picked up the broken shafted spade from the store.

"Stick the blade in the hinge," I told him. "See if it'll give."

They all looked at me. I wasn't supposed to tell people what to do but Skimp did it anyway and the rotten wood crumbled like a Flake bar.

Rocky took out his torch; he always had one with him. You never know when you might need one, he always said. I use mine for reading in bed at night when I'm not supposed to, but I could never see any need to carry it when I go to school every day or to the dinner table or get on the bus. Why would you carry a torch around with you unless one day you expected to go into a haunted house?

"Give me the torch," Mark said.

"It's my torch," said Rocky.

"But right now, I should have it," Mark insisted.

"This is a Maglite. Do you know how much

it costs? No way. I'll be point," he said, and eased past Mark – because going first is what being point means. I put a hand on Mark's arm, and nodded. Let Rocky do what he wants, he's seen more war films than us and he's brilliant at *Call of Duty*.

Besides, I thought this wasn't a good time to argue because ghosts, as everyone knows, can pick up vibrations in the air and if you start shouting that's like ringing the school bell for break. There would be ghosts coming out the woodwork to see what all the fuss was about.

As it happened we didn't need the torch once we got deeper into the house. The door we'd gone through led us into a kind of wash house that was attached to the side of the kitchen, a bit like Mum's utility room, but there were no washing machines, just big slabs of granite work counters and deep square sinks. This must have been where the servants did all the scrubbing. Mum says she needs domestic help with all our dirty washing, because she never knows how our clothes get so filthy. I always thought it was fairly obvious. It's because we play in places like Sweet Dreams Sweet Factory and haunted houses. Though to be honest this was the first haunted house I'd ever been in.

Skimp turned on a tap and there was a horrendous gurgling and rattling; the pipes shook and a deep, low groan echoed through the house. Skimp nearly fell over backwards in shock; the rest of us froze in fear.

"You idiot! What are you doing?" Pete-the-Feet shouted at him.

Skimp got such a fright that he shouted back. "Don't yell at me! I'm thirsty. I wanted a drink! I couldn't help it!"

"SHUSH!" the rest of us hissed.

The pipes settled into a long sigh. We waited and held our breath. Apart from the occasional clunk the pipes didn't make any more noise. We tiptoed forward. There was enough light coming around the edges of the boarded windows to show us a doorway. We all stood and waited. None of us was too keen to go any further. I heard thumping – but it was just my heart. But there was another sound. A groan. It was as if we'd stepped inside and stood on something that hurt. The house. It was the house that was groaning – that was why it was condemned.

Rocky put his torch on anyway.

A corridor with wood-panelled walls disappeared into the darkness and a big staircase went up from the hallway, which had nice big black and white tiles. They were just like the tiles Dad had tried to lay in our front porch, but he got the sizes a bit wrong when he cut them so instead of being black and white diamonds they ended up being more like different sized rectangles.

There was just enough light to see up the wooden stairs, which creaked under my feet. The staircase was so wide you could have carried a grand piano up it. There wasn't much light up there – the stairs just got swallowed by the gloom. There were marks on the walls, brown stains that showed where pictures had once hung. It was as if someone's faded memories had been stolen. Suddenly the house felt very sad.

Have you ever just wandered off? You're so entangled in your brain, thinking about lots of different things all at the same time that you suddenly don't know how you got to where you are.

I stopped dead in my tracks. One foot hovered over the next step.

There was something up there.

It sounded like a little whisper. Like rat's breath.

Whispers can be very damaging to your nervous system.

"Beanie!" Mark hissed.

I gasped.

I was halfway up the stairs. Another dozen steps and I'd have been in the murk. The others were going into another room that led off the corridor.

"Come on!" And he had that look that said he would kill me if I didn't get back to the rest of them.

I jumped down most of the stairs. Mark grabbed me.

"Do. Not. Go. Off. On. Your. Own," he said threateningly, his mouth close to my ear. If I hadn't been wearing my beanie he'd have sprayed all over me.

"There's something upst—"

But he pulled me into the room before I could tell him. Maybe it was better that I didn't say anything. Panic can be a terrible thing. But I lifted one edge of the beanie so I could listen for any more sounds from the darkness upstairs.

It was a very old-fashioned room. There were more missing memories on the walls and the floorboards moaned every time we took a step.

The thin line of light from the edge of the windows showed dust floating in the air.

Big old chairs sat on a threadbare rug that must have had a nice flower design on it at one time. A coffee table with spindly legs was in the middle and they were all nestled round the fireplace. But someone had ripped out the mantelpiece – it was probably marble like the one in the Civic Hall – and so now there was just bare brick and the black hole of the grate. If you thought about it long enough that could be a portal to the Underworld. Sometimes it's not a good idea to have a vivid imagination like mine. Dad says I could be a politician with the stories I tell.

There were two old cups and saucers on the coffee table and a book lay open, as if whoever had been reading it had been interrupted and left the room. The book was called *The History of Lacemaking*. That's something we've never touched on in Mrs Carpenter's class, but I suppose lacemaking never had much effect on the world, not like real history – wars and stuff and plagues. Though I have seen pictures of knights in the Crusades with chain mail, and who knows, maybe that came about because someone saw some old lady making lace, and thought, That's a good idea. Instead of a lace doily I'll make some arrow-resistant chain mail…

"Jez!" Mark tugged my sleeve. "Stop daydreaming! Come on."

Candyfloss cobwebs reached down from the ceiling; bookcases, still with loads of books on them, were thick with dust. I remember Mrs Carpenter, our teacher, who is, by the way, a very good storyteller – she does all the ups and downs in her voice when she reads, that's called intonation – she did a class project about a ghost ship. When people went on board there was still food on the table and drink in the cups, but no sign of anyone on board. That's how this was. Eerie and ghostly and a bit weird. I thought the place would have been empty of furniture. I suddenly felt as though I was in someone's lounge and I almost shouted, "Is there anybody home?"

But I didn't, just in case someone answered.

I picked up the book and blew the dust off it. Sometimes in the front of books the person whose book it is writes their name. Sometimes there's what they call a bookplate, which says Ex Libris. This one had a piece of paper stuck in the front with lots of dates stamped on it. The last one was 1988. It was a library book and it was overdue by twenty-five years.

What happened next was definitely not my fault. Old houses have woodworm, everyone knows that. They scoff all the timbers in the house. Sometimes you can't see where. So when I put the book back on the shelves – I did it without even thinking – they swayed for a second. When you see a film about a ship sinking and everything leans to one side – that's what this was like. I thought I was having another faint, but it wasn't me falling down, it was those hundreds of books.

It was an avalanche of books and I nearly got smothered.

Everyone jumped and shrieked.

"Beanie!"

"It wasn't me!" I shouted, but we were choking on the cloud of dust billowing up from the disintegrated bookshelves.

Rocky was crouching, Pete-the-Feet was behind his hair, Skimp was scrunched down with his hands over his head as if the roof was caving in and Mark was…

Suddenly, Mark pulled himself out of the dust

and mountain of books. I think it was the top shelf and the complete 1947 edition of *Encyclopaedia Britannica* that had rendered him momentarily unconscious. He staggered a bit, choked and coughed and pointed at me. But before he could say anything Skimp hissed.

"Sshhhhh. What's that?"

If someone could have taken a photograph right at that moment it would have shown the five of us frozen stiff, eyes wide, knees bent ready to run, and mouths open.

We held our breath.

Nothing.

"I don't hear anything," Rocky whispered.

"No. Me neither," said Mark. "It must have been the—"

Suddenly there was a rapid series of thumps across the ceiling. Someone running! Something was up there! And then it screamed! It was a scream that would have made the hairs on the back of my neck stand up – if I'd had any. Thump-thump-thump. The creature was pounding down the stairs.

I don't know who yelled first, it makes no difference, we ran like demented sheep.

That's known as panic.

And then suddenly I was in the dark. I'd turned the wrong way. I was on my own. I tripped and fell headlong into the dark passage. I was trapped. And I could hear the creature from the haunted house getting closer.

I was nine years, eleven months and nine days old, and I wanted to be ten.

5

Mark told me later that they didn't miss me until they got on the other side of the gates and by then it was nearly dark. There was a brief Emergency Meeting of the Executive Council about why I wasn't with them.

Legs chewed off seemed to be the best answer.

Then: why I hadn't screamed like them?

Swallowed head first seemed the most likely reason.

Then: what to do?

Brotherly love can only be expected to go so far. That's not to say Mark wasn't worried, he was – he had to think of what to tell Mum and Dad. He said he'd told them that I was sleeping over at Skimp's, who's got a new X-Box. And Mum had said she hoped I wasn't playing any violent video games.

He promised her I wasn't.

Whatever it was scuffled like a huge rat and I could hear it snorting. Maybe Peacock's Feather had been in here breeding and had created a monster beyond description. It probably drooled blood and ate any living flesh it could find. I held my breath. It was just there at the end of the dark patch where the light filtered down the stairs. I couldn't see it because it had edged into the darkness. All I could hear was my heart pounding away in my chest trying to find a way out. Then something in the darkness moved. I pushed my shoulders back against an old door – and pushed – and pushed!

It gave way and I was suddenly in another part of the big old country house kitchen. Moonlight slanted through a skylight high in the ceiling. Huge wooden tables and big slate floors made it look like a medieval torture chamber. I scrabbled backwards as fast as I could, keeping my eyes on the open door, and then I heard it coming! I closed my eyes. And screamed! Then I fell like a bag of cement and felt the wind whistle out of me. That really hurt, and I kept my eyes tightly closed. If I couldn't see it, then it might not see me.

Then it was on me.

In an instant I decided to play dead. If it thought I was as dead as a pork chop it might not tear me to pieces. But I couldn't stop screaming. Then I realised it wasn't me making all that noise – it was the monster. Screaming and chattering and howling like a mad monkey in a zoo.

It *was* a monkey!

A flat-nosed hairy face with big brown eyes was sniffing me and its breath was worse than Peacock's Feather's. I looked at it and it looked at me. I think it was more frightened than I was. Though I wouldn't like to take bets on that.

Me terrified.

Chimpanzee terrified.

Words were trying to come out my mouth, but they couldn't connect with my brain, and I heard myself say: "My name is Beanie and I won't hurt you. I promise." As if I could do anything – it was sitting on my chest and had a very peculiar smell, a bit like a wet dog who has rolled in something not that nice.

The chimpanzee's teeth grinned down at me, its lips pulled back, and then it made funny *whoo whoo whoo* sounds and screamed again. I nearly wet myself.

Then it jumped off me and drummed the floor with its feet and hands. I still couldn't escape because it was between me and the door. I sat up and gently edged towards the big table legs. I thought if I tried to run it would just jump on my back and bite my head off. So I decided the best course of action was to be as quiet as possible and hope it didn't hear my heart beating as loudly as its hands on the floor. I promise you it was so loud we could have had a drumming session together.

It stopped and looked at me. It seemed a little nervous. Its eyes darted around the room but kept coming back to me, checking me out, seeing if I was going to... do what? Attack it? Neither of us moved. I smiled as bravely as I could.

It pulled back its lips and bared its teeth. So did I. I thought that if I did what it did it might not attack me and it might understand how scared I was. The monkey looked at me and put its hand over its face and peeped through its fingers. So did I. Then it drummed the stone floor again with the palms of its hands and made a screeching noise. So I tried that as well. The monkey seemed to go a bit berserk. It did a couple of back flips, a tumble, rolled over on its head and sat down again looking at me. I didn't think I could manage that.

Suddenly it stood up, raised its arms above its head and grabbed an old soup ladle and started banging it against the cupboards. I got the fright of my life, an even bigger fright of my life than the fright of my life I had before, because I thought it was going to attack me like a mad axe man, only this was a mad chimpanzee with a ladle. I yelled in fright. The monkey jumped, dropped the ladle and ran screeching across the work counters and tables in the kitchen, then disappeared out through a door at the other end of the room.

Me being so scared had scared it.

Then I suddenly felt terrible. I stood up and shouted after it, "Wait! Don't go! It's all right! Honest!" I could hear it scuffling as it ran in the darkness where bits of moonlight broke up the dark like a splintered mirror. And for some reason I went after it without even thinking that it might have a bigger brother somewhere in there who might not even be a chimpanzee, but a gorilla. But my brain called me stupid and reminded me that chimpanzees and gorillas aren't the same. I could just make out the shapes of the worktops and the preparation tables in this huge kitchen. As I banged into things and tried to reach the door I had to pull a couple of cobwebs out of my face – which made me cringe – the thought of spiders did occur to me. Especially if one got into my beanie and worked its way underneath and decided to make a nest in my ear. I could have millions of tiny spiders being born inside my head and the only thing they would have to eat would be my brain. But that was an irrational thought because there was no chance a spider could get under my beanie because it was tighter than a cosy on Mum's teapot.

By the time I had stumbled through the kitchen I seemed to have come right round the back of the house again and I could see there was a huge cobbled courtyard with old stables and outhouses. I went down the passageway past broken windows where the boarding had rotted and given way, perhaps this was how the monkey had got inside the house. I could hear it still chattering, still running, still making lots of noise, and that's what I followed, until I finally came to a room that had lots of old clay garden pots stacked on the floor. There was a rotten wooden door leading into a huge greenhouse. It was like a jungle in there. Plants had just kept growing year in, year out, self-seeding fruit and vegetables, but there wasn't much left to eat that I could see. Whatever had been in here must have kept the monkey alive. Its very own private jungle. This would have made a great HQ.

I was getting really tired and sat on a pile of sacks. I remembered they called these big old Victorian greenhouses orangeries. But I couldn't see any oranges anywhere. The place smelled very musty, but most of the glass was still in the old frames and I supposed the big house would have once grown its vegetables there, because they wouldn't have had a supermarket in those days. The moonlight came through the cracked glass and cobwebs and made a big lace curtain over everything. It was very pretty. And it was quiet. The monkey had stopped making any noise. Sometimes, no matter what's going on, you just can't keep your eyes open and I started to snuggle down into the sacks but then they popped open again when I saw the monkey sitting in front of me. It was just watching. I remembered I had a Juicy Fruit in my pocket. I carefully took the paper off and held it out. The thought of it made my mouth water but I wanted to make a peace offering. The monkey's eyes widened and then suddenly it snatched the sweet from my fingers. It made a slobbering slurping chewing noise and then stuck its tongue out. The Juicy Fruit had made it red and I could smell the fruit on its breath, which was quite a bit better than what it smelled like before. I didn't move, just sat there and looked at it. It reached out and touched my foot. I kept quite still and slowly put my hand out to it again, just with my palm open.

It touched it and then I noticed for the first time that it had a plastic medical bracelet on its wrist. "Look," I said, "I've got one of those."

The chimpanzee gazed at me and then opened the palm of its hand. Using two fingers of its other hand it pretended to scoop up make-believe food into its mouth. It was talking to me! Telling me it was hungry. I had found a monster in the haunted house and it was asking for my help. How great was that? This was a secret worth more than anything.

"I'm going to find you some food. And I'm not going to tell anyone about you, but I have to go home now. I'll come back tomorrow. I promise."

The monkey chattered its teeth and covered its eyes.

"Don't be scared," I whispered. "I'll look after you."

By the time I managed to get out of the Black Gate the moon was high and the frost had settled like skin on a rice pudding. It seemed like ages to get home but it only took me about half an hour and I could see Mark peering out the window looking down our street. I waved and I saw him disappear. The next thing I knew he was waiting for me outside the front door, shivering. What did he expect? He only had his pyjamas on.

"You were at Skimp's playing on his X-Box. So don't forget!"

I pushed him.

"What was that for?" he moaned.

"You left me at the Black Gate!"

"We were going to come back for you later tonight. We had to wait till everybody was in bed. What was I supposed to tell Mum and Dad? I got into enough trouble when you did your factory stunt. This time they'd have killed me!"

I thought I'd better play it up a bit and make him feel as bad as I could. Besides, I didn't want any of them going back and finding my secret. "There's something really terrible in there. It was howling and moaning and scraping around. I bet it's some sort of alien creature that crawled out the sewer."

"You saw it!"

"It was huge. And it had bits of entrails all over it. It definitely wasn't human."

He looked at me as if he didn't believe me. Maybe I'd overdone it by mentioning entrails.

He nodded and pulled me in the front door. "Don't forget what I told you."

"Is that you, Jez?" Mum shouted from the kitchen. She popped her head around the corner as I was taking off my coat and shoes. "There you are," she said. "I was wondering if we were ever going to see you again. We thought you'd left home," she teased. "I've got your favourite, beans on toast."

Delish. "And I'd like an apple," I said.

She looked at me for a couple of seconds and said, "All right."

Anyone would think I had never asked for an apple before – though I admit I hadn't ever asked for one after beans on toast. She kept looking at me as if she wanted to find out why I had really asked for an apple. I wondered if she could smell the monkey, because she wrinkled her nose a bit, but she does that when she's thinking.

"It's a strange time of day to want an apple," she said. "Are you feeling all right?" She put her hand on my forehead just below my beanie. "You're quite hot," she said.

"That's because I've been running, Mum," I told her.

And then she did that pretend thing where she doesn't realise that I know what she's really thinking.

"So you were at Rocky's," she said as she poured the beans onto the toast.

I started cutting up the soggy bread and getting as much as I could inside my mouth so that she couldn't tell when I was lying. When you're concentrating on your food and your mouth is full, parents are easily fooled anyway. "No, I was at Skimp's."

She nodded. *Just testing*, I could almost hear her brain say.

I think it's a sad day when your own mother doesn't trust you.

That's called having a suspicious mind.

Everything you Need to Know in the World says that chimpanzees are very intelligent creatures and prefer a balanced diet. Beans on toast is not considered part of their daily nourishment requirements. Fruit, nuts, seeds and insects is what they need for strong bones and healthy gums. I think I can manage everything except the insects – they can be difficult to catch in any quantity. Chimps prefer dense tropical rainforests but can also be found in secondary-growth forests, woodlands, bamboo forests, swamps, and even open savannah, the book tells me. That must be why he likes the old greenhouse, I bet it gets steaming hot in there during the day. I suppose I could always put Mum's rubber plant in the bathroom for him and keep the shower going for some steam. Mum always says it's like a sauna when I'm in there. And I could take him to Childwall Woods so he could do a bit of swinging on branches or I might be able to sneak him into Centre Parcs when we go on our holiday next year.

I don't think I can manage a bamboo forest, though, unless we could sneak him into the garden centre one night – they've got a bit of a patch there. I bet Dad will think of something when I eventually make the introductions. I don't know that there are too many swamps around here. The canal is a bit rough, what with all the junk thrown in it, so we might have to give up on the swamp idea. Other than that I think we could manage.

Apparently, chimps can grow to over a metre tall and like being in family groups of five or six. That might work then. Once we get a better understanding between us I could bring him home and he could be like my younger brother. Then, with Mum and Dad and me and Mark, he would have the perfect family. But first I have to make sure that he would be happy with that arrangement. I don't really know what chimpanzees think of us human beings. *Everything you Need to Know in the World* did tell me that chimpanzees are quite territorial and they like to have their own patch in the jungle, and that if anyone strays in or out of it, that can cause problems with their neighbours. I'm thinking of Mrs Tomkinson in these circumstances. I can just hear her screaming: "Get that flaming monkey off my washing line!" Suddenly I feel a great sense of responsibility towards him. He's small, he's scared and he needs help. He is also an endangered species. And I'm the only one who can save him.

I'd made some progress. I got an extra banana in my lunchbox from Mum and that, with the apple from last night, was a start. Mark didn't stop asking questions all the way to school. He thought I wasn't, as he put it, traumatised enough. I should have been a gibbering idiot after seeing the monster and being trapped in the Black Gate.

"I had terrible nightmares all night," I told him.

"Really?" he said. "Bad ones?" He seemed pleased.

"They were terrifying. I woke up sweating at least twice. The creature was really horrible. I don't even want to talk about it, it was so scary."

"That's called Post Traumatic Stress Syndrome," Rocky said. "You'll probably have those nightmares for the rest of your life. They never go away. Sometimes you'll be walking down the street and you suddenly see the monster when he's not really there."

"Shut up, you!" Mark said.

"It's a well-known fact that children can overcome

stressful situations and lead a normal happy life," Pete-the-Feet said.

Skimp picked his nose and studied the results before flicking it away. "We breathe in all kinds of muck these days. Pollution is only one thing to worry about. Beanie might have inhaled alien spores. By the time we get to school they might be germinating inside him. He could become a hive, a carrier of unknown creatures."

"Don't talk rot, Skimp. Most of what Jez saw was in his imagination. There are no aliens in the Black Gate," said Mark.

"There was a monster! You heard it!" I said, thinking I had better keep them scared enough to stay away from the house.

"With entrails," Mark said sarcastically.

"Absolutely," I told him. "Horrible. I'm never going anywhere near that place again," I said. Then I ran into school, grateful that I could escape into Mrs Carpenter's class about the many wives of Henry the Eighth. It's only the chopping off of heads bit that's interesting.

The government, whoever they are, seem to feel a

personal responsibility for me. Anyone would think they're like teachers or Mum and Dad, because they recommend that I eat five essential fruits and vegetables every day. So when it comes to lunchtime, it doesn't matter what I have in my box from Mum, I have to line up and have a hot meal. The dinner ladies, especially Mrs Hutchins, have special instructions to make sure I get all the greens. I have complained that I could get vegetablitis but it seems to be some sort of golden rule that Jez Matthews has to have everything, so she piles them on. And she's been told that I have to have extra broccoli. Sometimes that's difficult, especially when it comes to broccoli. No one in their right mind likes broccoli. No sooner is it on your plate than it goes cold. And this is supposed to be a hot meal. That's called a contradiction. But I have to eat lots of it, so Mum says, because it's full of iron. Which makes me wonder that if I could get enough down me that I could end up like Iron Man.

If broccoli's supposed to be so wonderful I wonder how my chimpanzee had managed for so long without eating this stuff. Then I saw Jenny Moffat scoffing down broccoli like it was her last meal on earth.

"What are you doing?" I asked her, though it was quite obvious.

Jenny Moffat is a well-brought-up girl and never speaks with her mouth full. She also chews a lot. And when she's finished chewing she cleans her teeth with her tongue and then speaks to you. As I said, she's a very polite girl.

"Hello Beanie," she said. "How's your head?"

"It's fine. Sometimes it gets a bit hot. So," I asked her again, "what are you doing? With the broccoli."

"I can't stand the stuff," she said. "But I know I have to eat it because my mum said it will make me beautiful when I grow up. So the best thing to do is to eat it first and get it out the way, then I can eat the rest of food that I really like."

I thought that was a very sensible thing to do. It's a bit like when Dad says don't put off what you're supposed to do today until tomorrow. "Get it out the way, then you can play!"

"Would you like my broccoli, because then you could be even more beautiful than you're planning to be? In fact, you might even become a supermodel, because I know they live off vegetables and salads."

"Is that true?"

"Absolutely. I read it. You could have my broccoli if I could have your banana."

She considered it for a moment and then nodded. I scraped my broccoli onto her plate and tucked her banana into my backpack. This was an extremely good deal. I was going to make her the most beautiful woman in the world and I hadn't had to eat the broccoli or exchange my Snickers Bar, which, as a trading currency, holds great value.

By the time lunch break was over I had managed to secure two more apples, another banana, an orange and a fruit bar. I sacrificed my chips for the apple, and my raspberry yoghurt for the orange, but I could only get a fruit and nut bar for my Snickers, which wasn't a great deal. It looked a bit soggy and sticky, and I thought that the fruit and nuts might get stuck in the chimpanzee's teeth and as he couldn't go to the dentist, I ate it. Then I didn't feel as dizzy, but I was picking bits of stuff out my teeth for ages.

I know I have to eat something or I get a bit faint, I think that's because of all the medicine I take, but I'm on a mission to get as much food as possible for my new friend. Mark always tells me to eat a banana whenever I can because that's a good energy food. Just like the tennis players at Wimbledon, and the footballers, and long-distance runners, and rugby players, and soldiers, and round the world yachtsmen, and mountain climbers and... the list goes on. I sometimes wonder if there can possibly be enough bananas in the whole world – maybe that's why chimpanzees are an endangered species, because we are all sports-mad and eating their bananas. I think I should start a new campaign for all those people to eat a chocolate bar instead.

Save the World – Eat a Chocolate Bar!

6

I sneaked out, scared that Mark might see me, but then I saw him and the others in the chemistry lab. They were wearing goggles as they stood around something that looked as though it was going to burst into flames at any minute. I sometimes think teachers are either very brave or very stupid – I wouldn't let Rocky near anything potentially explosive.

I thought that no one would miss me if I didn't hang about for the Design and Technology class where we were going to design and make a pair of slippers. That would be very useful, I suppose, if you were planning to be a care worker in an old people's home, but I had to save a frightened and starving chimpanzee, so there was no contest. I'll apologise now for all the elderly people who will need slippers one day.

I was very careful about going back to the Black

Gate, because although everyone thought it was haunted and infested by evil spirits there was always the possibility that other kids would take as big a risk as we had. I crept into the bushes near the main gates and waited, then eased through the side of the gate, and pushed the bits of bush and weeds back into the gap. It was still a bit nerve-racking going up to the house, because you never knew what else could be up there. I mean, if the chimpanzee had been dumped by someone who kept exotic pets because they couldn't afford to feed him any more, then there might be all kinds of creatures lurking. What if there were snakes or crocodiles? I hadn't been into any of the bathrooms yet, so who knew what might be in there?

I sneaked in the same way. I stopped and listened. The house was still as gloomy as it had been the day before and I couldn't hear anything – there were no obvious sounds of slithering crocodiles or bone-crushing snakes curled around the banister. I whispered as loudly as I could, "Hello, monkey?"

He didn't answer, but then I guessed he was probably still scared, but I hoped he might have recognised my voice. I moved further into the house and the floorboards squeaked no matter how carefully I trod. It was still very creepy. I whispered again, but there was no reply. Now I was getting a bit worried that after yesterday I had scared him off and he might have escaped. Then he'd be running around in the countryside, lost and confused with no idea where to go or where I lived. So there was no way he could come and get help from me.

I went into the kitchen again and through the back door to the courtyard and the big greenhouse. "Monkey? Monkey? It's me, Beanie. Remember me?" I listened but I still couldn't hear anything. I sat down on the old sacks and emptied the food from my backpack and kept talking to him all the time, hoping that he could hear me and that the sound of my voice would bring him out from wherever he was hiding.

"I've got a really nice big banana and a couple of apples and a very juicy orange as I'm sure you must be thirsty as well. I also brought a bottle of water with me from the canteen, but I ate the fruit and nut bar because that was really sticky and chewy."

I sat and waited with the food laid out in front of me like a car boot sale. The clouds were coming over and I knew it was going to rain and if I got home late and soaking wet Mum would have a fit, so I hoped Monkey was going to come out soon. I didn't want to just leave the food because if there were other creatures lurking in the tangled plants, which was something I didn't really want to think about too much, then he might not get anything to eat at all. I suppose I felt quite protective about him now; maybe that's how Mark feels about me.

Then I heard a rustle. I could just see his little round face peeping between the branches. "Hello, Monkey," I said very gently "It's me again, have you had a busy day?" I picked up a banana and held it out at arm's length. He was looking but I could see he was nervous. "This is a really good energy food, it'll be a great benefit to you for all the climbing you have to do, but I suppose you know that."

He came out from the bushes very slowly, looking left and right but kept glancing back at the banana – then he stopped and made little sort of cooing sounds. I held my breath – he was so close to me now I could have leaned forward and stroked his head – but I just stayed as still as I could. I was willing him to reach out and take the banana from my hand.

And then he did. Well, he didn't so much take it as
snatch it. And then he scuttled back under the leaves
and quickly ate the banana, even with the skin on.
Maybe he didn't know you were supposed to peel them
or maybe that's how chimpanzees eat them anyway. I
thought I had his attention now so I reached out and
put one of the apples at arm's length and sat back and
waited to see if he would come back and take it.

This time he seemed a bit more relaxed as he
edged forward on all fours, his front knuckles
scraping the floor. He stopped and sat and looked
at me. My heart was beating so fast I couldn't think
of anything to say so I said something really stupid.
"Tennis players eat bananas all the time." As if that
was going to make any sense to him at all and he
certainly wasn't going to take up tennis as a sport,
was he? He made a couple of signs with his hands
but I don't know what he was doing. But they were
very definite movements. I tried to copy them but
he just looked at me as if I was daft. We both sat
looking at each other so I carefully picked up the
apple and took a bite. Then I handed the rest of it to
him. He took it and ate it and if Jenny Moffat had
seen him she'd have had a fit.

He squatted down, scratched his bum and chewed with his mouth open, which I suppose are perfectly acceptable table manners in the jungle. He rolled his head around looking up at the glass, where the tapping of the rain attracted his attention. He scratched again and then carefully stretched out his arm for the orange.

"They're full of vitamin C," I told him, "though if you eat too many you can get the trots. I'm not sure how many but probably a few dozen. Dad squeezes me fresh oranges every Sunday morning because that's his one day off. He's a postman."

I wasn't sure whether he was listening to me or not. He kept looking at me and nodding his head as he peeled away the orange skin and then carefully pulled away each segment of the orange. That's called dexterity. He seemed quite interested in what I was saying, though I knew he couldn't understand, but perhaps the tone of my voice held his attention. I tried to read what it said on his medical band but the writing was smudged and faded.

He picked orange bits out of his teeth. I was convinced he was really smiling at me. In about five minutes I told him everything about myself,

Mum and Dad, and Mark, about how he was going to play for Liverpool FC, as Michael Owen used to and Steven Gerrard does, because he's brilliant. And about the gang and me, and about when I got sick and had to start going to hospital and just how much Mum gets upset, and Dad too, of course, but that what I have can be treated, though it made all my hair fall out, which is why I wear a beanie.

I took it off and lowered my head. "Look, see? Nothing. Not like you, you hairy monkey." I laughed and Monkey looked at me and then, and this is amazing, and no one will ever believe this, but he reached out a hand and touched my head. He made that chattering noise again and put his hand on his own head. His eyes widened and he gave that big toothy grin and rolled over backwards. "Whoo whoo," he said. So I made the same noise. And then I rolled over. He rubbed his hands over his face, then chattered. Then he pointed at me and patted his chest. I didn't know what he meant so I did the same – pointing at him.

I think we might have had a conversation.

"I have to think of a name for you," I told him as I handed over the last piece of fruit. Names are very important. Dad once told me that they create an image in people's minds. Like Silver Surfer, Batman, Spider Man – though his real name is Peter Parker – in fact, lots of superheroes have their own names. Clark Kent for Superman, Bruce Wayne for Batman, Norrin Radd for the Silver Surfer and Bruce Banner was the Hulk. Even I've got two names. Jez Matthews and Beanie. Dad told me, after all my hair fell out, that by wearing the beanie I was like a superhero, and that all the horrible things some kids said just wouldn't penetrate the Power of the Beanie. And he was right.

So what about Monkey?

I watched his face: "Ricky, Mickey, Mikey, Mo?"

He screeched and chattered. Rain dribbled from the broken panes. Okay, maybe they didn't have a certain ring to them. "Charlie, Chatty, Chippy, Chez, Clyde, Claude, Clint?"

He went ape! Head back, teeth bared, lips pouting, hands beating the floor.

"All right," I said. "Those are the coolest names I can think of right now."

Monkey nodded and rubbed his head. Then the second most wonderful thing happened. It was getting late and the rain was chucking it down, so I had to get home. I stood up and said to him very quietly: "I have to go home now but I'll come back tomorrow. Miss Sanderson has a dance class but I'm excused so no one will miss me." And then – as I started to walk away – he held my hand.

I felt this wave of something inside me. It was as if he wanted me to look after him like a little child who was lost and had found someone he trusted. Then I felt terrible. What could I do? There was no way I could take him home.

"I'll... make a plan... I will... I'll find a way to take you home. I promise," I stammered.

Just then a gust of wind slammed an old window frame. It was so loud and unexpected that we both jumped with fright. He made a screeching noise and ran off on all fours into the bushes. I almost followed him but realised that if he was scared he would stay inside the greenhouse hiding in the plants, and that was the best thing for him. So I said quietly, really to myself, "I promise I won't leave you here for ever. You'll see."

Mark had football practice so it was just Mum,

Dad and me for tea. Dad goes to bed early because he has to get up at four in the morning to go and sort his mail. After that he loads the trolley or his bike and starts his round. Sometimes there's so much mail they have to take more bags of letters and leave them at people's houses as pick-up points. Then, when Dad has finished doing one route, he picks up the extra stuff and starts again. I don't know how he manages to do that, but it's all because of our circumstances. Between Mum and Dad they try to make sure there's always someone at home for me.

There's a bit of a routine in our house. Once we've eaten, I do my homework while they watch the telly. Then we watch a film or something they've recorded. We're not allowed televisions in our rooms like a lot of kids, especially me, because I am not supposed to get overtired and if I had one in my room they know I'd be watching it half the night, at least that's what Dad says. And if they gave one to Mark then that wouldn't be fair. That's another thing that irritates him.

I don't really mind because I get to read a lot of different books and, better still, sometimes Dad takes half an hour before he goes to bed early and tells me a story or reads to me. He tells great stories, does my dad. When we used to go on the long-distance journeys he could tell a complete story between each service stop on the motorway. Sometimes I would see the sign telling us it was only six miles to the next service station and he was only halfway through a story, but by the time we roared past all those people getting out their cars to go and have a large cup of cappuccino and a brie baguette with lettuce and tomato, he would get to the end of the story. Amazing. How did he know when the ending was going to come?

You can forgive him being no good at DIY when you hear the stories he makes up. Or if he reads to me it's like going to a film. He does all the voices and even jumps around the room acting. In that respect he's even better than Mrs Carpenter, who's a bit limited when it comes to doing monsters' voices. "Don't get him excited!" Mum always calls up the stairs when she hears him. "He'll never get to sleep!"

And she's right, I often don't. Not for ages. Not with all that stuff in my head. It would probably be better for me having a telly.

It was while I was chewing my way through

Mum's lasagne that the next part of my plan came into my head. What a monkey needed was someone to keep him company until he became comfortable having humans around. That's called socialising. And obviously that someone had to be me. So for the first time ever, I had to start planning a way of getting out of classes and spending more time at the Black Gate. I could never forge Mum's or Dad's handwriting for a note, so I had to find something else. By the time we got to the tinned fruit pudding I had worked it all out.

If Mark found out that I had messed with his computer I think he would stop me from ever becoming a full-time member of his gang. But helping Monkey was even more important than that. Mum always kept my hospital appointment letter stuck on the fridge with a magnetic picture of a grizzly bear and its cub. While Dad was washing the dishes and watching the sports news on the kitchen telly I slid the letter from underneath the grizzly bear mum's claws.

Once you've scanned something into a computer you can then save it in a letter file. Then you can type over the date you're supposed to go for your appointment. And when you've printed it out you've got a new letter with a new date to give it to your class teacher excusing you from their lesson. I had to spend as much time as possible with Monkey so I thought every afternoon for a week would be a good idea to pretend to have a hospital appointment. So I typed in five different dates but used the same time for the appointment.

Then I switched everything off, made sure I took the original hospital letter from Mark's multifunction printer, which had been a very good price from Bad Boys Computer Emporium, and put it back on the fridge when Mum and Dad were sitting down in the lounge watching *Britain's Got Talent*, with Mum shouting at the judges.

7

Sometimes being scared or nervous can work in your favour. When I handed the letter to Mrs Donovan, our music teacher, the next day she read it and had quite a sad look on her face. And then she smiled and put a hand on my shoulder and said, "I'm sorry you're going to miss singing today, Jez. It's your favourite."

We've been practising 'He's Got the Whole World in His Hands' for the end of term concert. She bent down and held my shoulders and said, "It'll be all right, Jez. We'll do it again next week so you don't miss it."

She is very caring, is Mrs Donovan, and I felt a bit bad for deceiving her. But I had to get to Monkey and save him and that was more important than anything else. Sometimes you have to give up things that are important to you so you can help someone else. Even singing my favourite song. Well, second favourite if you count 'You'll Never Walk Alone'.

Getting into Black Gate was less creepy now. It felt a bit like going into your own house. You know where the doors are, you know where the kitchen is. Of course, I hadn't had a chance to explore the whole house yet, it was still very dark in most of the rooms and there were still shadows that tended to take on different shapes if I looked at them too long. So it was quite helpful to sing the words of the song to myself as I made my way through to the big greenhouse.

When I emptied my backpack this time I had lots of treats for Monkey. I sat on the sacks and laid out books to read to him, some comics, a packet of fruit and nuts, some Juicy Fruits and a T-shirt, because I thought that, even though he was a chimpanzee, he might be getting a bit cold at this time of year.

I sat on the sacks and waited. As soon as he heard my voice he came out of hiding and, without even asking, took an apple, and sat right in front of me, as if we were in class together and were going to do a reading project.

I thought I should keep it simple to start with, so while he crunched away at the apple I started reading from one of my favourite stories about a boy in Africa who makes friends with a lion and then a terrible thing happens and the lion gets sent to a zoo and then the boy becomes a soldier and when he's fighting in France he sees the lion in the cage and they are reunited.

But after about a page and a bit the monkey seemed more interested in picking his toenails, which my mum would think was a pretty disgusting thing to do while you are eating.

"It's a very good story and I think you'll find the relationship between the lion and the boy is very similar to you and me," I told him. But then I remembered when I first went to school that the teacher had taught us all to read using picture books, so I took out one of the comics I had brought with me. That way I could describe the picture and show him.

"This is the Silver Surfer, who travels faster than the speed of light. See, there's the Silver Surfer zooming across the sky and he is about to go into battle with Doomsday Man."

Every time I explained the picture I showed it to him. He looked, grinned and made that funny noise with his lips again, so I think he was getting the hang of it. Once he had finished the banana, he got up and did a head over heels roll, which I think was his way of telling me he was happy. And then he walked back towards the kitchen, stopped and looked at me, as if he was waiting for me to join him. So I did.

He scuttled off through the darkened kitchen and back into the hallway. I followed him through the hall, stepping in and out of those creepy shadows and listening as the wind came through the old window frames.

He chatted and scampered up the stairs, but I wasn't too sure that I wanted to go up there. There are times when having an imagination is a really bad thing, because what looks like an old light-fitting can suddenly become a snake's head. The best thing to do in that situation is to tell your brain to shut up – you know it's only a light fitting and it would have to be something supernatural to turn it into a bone-crushing snake. By the time I told my brain to stop being so stupid I was at the top of the stairs looking down a long passageway that was big enough to have old pieces of furniture in it.

Monkey was already halfway down the corridor,

standing in the shadows. This is where my brain finally won because it was quite obvious that this passageway was the entrance to a monster's tomb, and, if I walked on those creaking floorboards and opened any of these doors, creatures from another world were bound to devour me. I started singing in my head.

When you walk through a storm,
Hold your head up high,
And don't be afraid of the dark…

Sing it louder, I shouted at myself without a sound. Try another song. Maybe it was better to sing something aloud.

"He's got the whole world in His hands, He's got the whole wide world in his hands…" That was more of a whisper than singing.

By this time the monkey had scuttled back and tugged at my anorak. Then he ran off again, jumping on the tatty old sofas and chairs, making a real game of it. When your brain doesn't work properly because you're so scared, you have to try and see things for what they are. There was Monkey playing down the corridor of death. Right in front of the monster's tomb. So obviously there was nothing scary down there. It was just me. Idiot me.

I ran after him and watched as he disappeared through an open door. When I went in I saw that this was where he slept. A threadbare carpet covered most of the floor and an iron bedstead with a mattress was pushed against one wall. There was a stain on the other side where it looked as though a big wardrobe had once stood. Tattered curtains hung the length of the tall windows, which had wooden shutters closed across them. And, although they had been boarded up from the outside, there was a small side window where the wooden shutters had fallen off. This was high above the bedstead, and this is where Monkey jumped up onto the sill. This was his lookout! I climbed up after him and, standing on tiptoe on the bed head, I could just see out. It was high enough to stop anyone breaking in, but I could see all the grounds, the courtyard and the greenhouses and the track that led around from the main gates, although you couldn't see the gates because they were hidden by all the trees. So from up here it looked as though there had once been a sweeping driveway that curved all the way round to the front of the house.

This was where he must have been when Mark's

gang and I came into the house and we heard him scurrying across the upstairs landing. Bits of ragged curtains and cushions from chairs were on the bed and it looked as though he had made his own nest. This was his bedroom and he was sharing it with me. It was like a very special den. Him and me – our own HQ!

I could imagine the house full of chandeliers, not just the old bits of wire that now hung down from the holes in the ceiling – and it was as if all those chandeliers suddenly came on all at once. Light glistened everywhere in my head because I knew that we were safe! If the monkey ran round without being scared then so could I. So I did.

I aeroplaned along the monster passageway and ran down the stairs and then back up again – until I was so tired I nearly fell asleep. The Black Gate was my castle and I was the king. No one would come here, this was my secret place.

The monkey chattered and bounced off the walls like a rubber ball and he could run twice as fast as me, but we ran together! By the time we got back to the big old greenhouse I was starting to shake. I shoved a banana into my mouth and drank some water and then just lay back on the sacks. I had to have a sleep and just before I closed my eyes Monkey sat next to me.

For some reason a name came into my head. It wasn't very cool, it wasn't very modern, nothing like a film star's name, but it just felt right. "Thank you, Malcolm, for showing me how not to be scared."

Malcolm Monkey just rubbed his head, scratched his bum and curled up next to me. He was warm, smelly and hairy – and I loved him.

"Uh!" I gasped. Malcolm had jumped off me and was beating the floor. I thought I'd been dreaming but there was the banana skin and the apple core and the comics. It was almost dark so I must have slept for a couple of hours, but Malcolm was frightened about something and ran off.

"Malcolm!" But he just ignored me.

I went after him and saw him scurrying up the stairs towards the bedroom. By the time I got there I was wheezing and I saw this lump under the cushions and curtains squirming. He was hiding from something, but what?

I climbed up on top of the bedstead and peeped

out the window. I could just see a splash of blue and yellow through the trees. It was a police car. I squashed my face against the window pane so I could see further and there was a white van parked just next to it.

I got a shock. There were three men walking down the track. Two were policeman and the other was an RSPCA inspector. One of them looked up and I fell back in fright. I landed on the bed and heard Malcolm screech. I burrowed under the covers and put my hand on his head and a finger to my lips. "Shush," I whispered. "There are people outside and they must be looking for you."

He burrowed deeper and I covered him with another piece of old lace curtain, then I climbed back up and peeped out the window again. I held my breath and tried to hear what the men were saying. I caught a few words: "No sign of entry in here... boarded up... ready to fall down... death-trap... not going in there, mate...'

I watched as they walked back into the trees. Malcolm must be a fugitive, wanted by the police. Why? What had he done? Or were they hunting him because he had escaped from somewhere?

I heard a car door slam and the engine start up. I listened so hard I thought my eardrums were going to pop, but I couldn't hear anything else. Maybe it was a trap. You know when the bad guys pretend to have left and the good guys come out but there are other bad guys waiting to snatch them? Watching films and reading books teaches you a lot about how horrible people behave. I waited a few minutes, but I still couldn't hear anything, so I decided to tiptoe out the room.

I got about halfway down the stairs along the creaking floorboards when I heard something. Someone was whispering. And there was a flash of light from a torch in the downstairs hall. I froze. My stomach felt as though I had swallowed a bucket of ice. The light jigged around and whispers were smothered by the old house as if I had cotton wool in my ears. I turned around and crept on all fours up the stairs to spread my weight and stop the floorboards from creaking. When I got to the upstairs corridor I walked as quickly as I could, went into the bedroom and closed the door, which *did* creak! My heart jumped. I clambered into bed and under the covers with Malcolm.

It was almost dark so I could barely see his face, but I could feel him trembling with fear – or was that just my hand shaking as I reached out to comfort him?

The muffled voices wafted up the stairs from the hall below. I had lifted my beanie above my ears so I could listen. Then I heard a familiar voice:

"Ouch!"

"Shut up, Skimp!" another hissed.

I scrambled out from under the covers and made my way to the stairs. It must be Mark and the gang. I was still quite nervous, you never know what kind of tricks bad people can play, but by the time I was halfway down the stairs I was sure who it was.

"Don't be an idiot. Get that light out my eyes!" said Rocky's voice.

"I'm here!" I called.

There was the sound of feet scrambling and by the time I got to the bottom of the stairs the gang was there.

"Beanie!" Pete-the-Feet said. And then screamed.

Skimp and Rocky nearly knocked each other over, and the torch dropped on the floor as Mark and Pete-the-Feet backed away, both of them banging into the wall, knocking over a table and ending up in a heap without taking their eyes off me.

Skimp was pointing at me with his mouth open wide.

I looked behind me. A small ghost had appeared. It was Malcolm with his arms raised, completely draped in the torn lace curtain.

Everyone yelled except me.

And when he made that *Whoo whoo whoo* noise – which to be fair does sound a bit ghost-like – they all curled up as if a monster had crept out the dungeons. Not that Black Gate had any dungeons – as far as I knew.

"It's all right," I told them. "Look, it's just Malcolm."

As I tugged the curtain off him Malcolm wrapped his arms around me like a scared baby.

"See? He won't hurt you. He's my friend."

People tend to state the obvious, so when they all saw Malcolm they pointed and said, "It's a monkey."

Then they got to their feet, but they didn't come any closer.

"Beanie, what's going on?" Skimp said.

Before I could say anything, Mark, who

was always braver than the rest of us, grabbed me by the front of my anorak "You should've—".

But before he could say anything else, Malcolm screeched and looked very threatening. Mark and the others backed off quickly. I soothed Malcolm and he held on to me again. "You mustn't scare him," I said. "He's very frightened and is very protective of me because I'm his friend."

"*He's* frightened?" Pete-the-Feet said. "Blimey, we were terrified."

"No, we weren't," said Rocky.

"You were so," Skimp said.

"Shut up, you two," Mark told them. "All right, Jez, what's going on?"

"Come on, I'll show you," I said and led them through into the big old greenhouse. Malcolm ran ahead and I smiled at the others but they didn't smile back.

I told them everything once they had all sat quietly and it didn't take long for Malcolm to be more relaxed. He sat next to me, of course, and made sure his shoulder touched mine. The others emptied their pockets and found anything edible. There wasn't much – a few sweets and a bar of chocolate – but they gave it to me and I gave it to Malcolm, because obviously he was a bit nervous of them and only trusted me.

"That's amazing," said Rocky. "You're really brave coming in here on your own. I think you should be made a full-time gang member."

"I second that," Pete-the-Feet said, pulling the hair back from his face.

"I think he should be banned completely," Mark said. He was scowling and sat with his arms around his knees. "He disobeyed all the rules of the gang, he kept a secret from us, and he put himself at risk by coming in here. He could have got hurt, he could have been attacked, the monkey might have rabies, anything could have happened. Then we would have got the blame."

Skimp had given Malcolm some chewing gum and was showing him how to chew it and pull it out in a long string, chew it again, and then blow bubbles. Malcolm was getting chewing gum in his fur and I had to help him before it all became matted. I was really using it as an excuse to think as fast as I could because Mark had the authority to expel me for ever and I have to admit he was right in everything he said, except that anybody who knows anything about chimpanzees knows they don't get rabies. They may have bad breath but that's as dangerous as it gets – and Mark isn't the best tooth cleaner around either.

"He was very frightened," I told them. "It took me ages to gain his confidence. I couldn't tell you because if we had all come in here he would have been terrified. Like the first time we came in. Imagine what it must feel like for him to have monsters like us coming out the dark."

"That's a fair point," Pete-the-Feet said. "We were the ones who invaded his territory."

"That's got nothing to do with it!" said Mark.

"Don't raise your voice. It makes Malcolm nervous," I said quietly.

"Whichever way you look at it," Rocky said quietly, which I thought was very considerate of him, "Beanie found the monkey, and the monkey likes him."

I could see the others were beginning to like the idea of having Malcolm around and that Mark might well have to agree to the democratic process again.

"He's doing things with his hands. What's that?" Rocky asked.

"I don't know. Sometimes he sits and does that," I told them.

"It's like sign language," Pete-the-Feet said.

"Like Native Americans?" Skimp asked.

"No, it's like that deaf kid, Tracy whatserface," Mark told them.

"Maybe he's deaf then," said Rocky.

"Don't be stupid, he heard us coming. It's monkey-see monkey-do. He's seen it somewhere, that's all," said Mark.

Skimp giggled. "He blew a bubble!"

Malcolm picked the chewing gum off his face and put it back into his mouth, but I think he also thought it was a lot of fun because he screeched and rubbed his hand across his head and did a back flip. Everyone laughed except Mark. But I think he could see which way the vote was going.

"Come on, Mark, we could look after him," Pete-the-Feet said.

"Yeah, there's bags of grub around. We could bring it in every day just like Beanie's been doing," Rocky said. "He deserves a chance and Beanie's been really gutsy. I say we form a special bodyguard unit to look after Malcolm."

They all looked at Mark. Malcolm chattered. I put my arm around him and scratched his head for him.

Mark shook his head in defeat. "Malcolm's a stupid name for a monkey."

"That's true," agreed Skimp.

"Skimp's not exactly great," I said.

"Also true," Skimp said.

"Malcolm is a nice name," I told them, "and it came to me out of nowhere. Just in a flash. That's called inspiration."

"That's called being off your head," Mark said. But then he gave in. "All right. I hereby declare that we are now the official bodyguard for Malcolm. We hereby promise to protect and feed him. We do solemnly swear."

"We do solemnly swear," we all said together.

And Malcolm blew another bubble.

8

While Mark and the others explored the rest of the house, being careful not to fall through any of the rotten floorboards, I could see that Malcolm needed sleep. He yawned and stretched and kept cuddling up to me.

I held his hand and walked upstairs and then to his bedroom. I showed him the T-shirt I had brought him but he didn't know what to do with it. So I took off my coat and my jersey and my own T-shirt. It was pretty cold but I thought that if it was true what Mark said about monkey-see and monkey-do then he would understand how to dress himself if I showed him.

He watched and pulled the T-shirt over his head. He couldn't find the armholes so I helped him and in next to no time he was ready for bed. I never thought I would have parted with my Steven Gerrard shirt but Malcolm needed it more than me.

He pulled his thumbs and hands down across his chest. I wasn't sure whether it was to smooth the shirt down or that he was making another one of those signs.

But I knew it was time to find out.

Once Malcolm was asleep we crept out the house, being very careful that there was no one around to see us. I was still nervous about the police and the RSPCA. We were still talking about it when two men pulled up in an old battered BMW. They looked really rough. One of them had a face like a potato, all lumpy with a couple of warts on it. The other had long, greasy hair, which was combed over a bald patch. They were both much older than my dad. We've always been told not to talk to strangers, but we didn't have much choice, because they stopped and wound down the window.

"Oi! You lads. Have you been down the Black Gate?" said Potato Face.

If you shove your hands in your pockets and look really disinterested most grown-ups ignore you anyway. Rocky pulled his hood up and Pete-the-Feet let the hair fall across his face.

"Nah. Why would we?" Mark said.

"I saw you hanging about down there. That's a dangerous site, that is. Whole thing could collapse at any minute," Comb Head said.

"We weren't doing anything," I said, because I was only nine years, eleven months and eleven days old, and grown-ups think I'm just an innocent child and tend to believe me.

"Listen, son, I'm not the law, I just want to know what you were doing in there."

"It's none of your business," Mark said.

"We're just kids," Skimp said.

Potato Face looked really mean but then he gave a sort of smile, which wasn't really a smile. I just think it's the way his face twisted when he wanted to try and appear nice. "Me, I don't care, about nothing. All I'm asking is, if you were in there, did you see anything unusual?"

"You can't get inside," Rocky said, "it's all boarded up. Besides, like you said, it's just too dangerous."

"What are you looking for?" I asked them.

He gave a sneer, and tapped the side of his nose. "Don't get too nosey, kid, it can be bad for your health."

He had no idea how often I went to hospital. That's called irony.

Tracy Lewis looked a bit weird. She wore ankle boots and black tights and a crinkly sort of skirt and she had bangles and beads and a purple cardigan that sort of matched the colour of her hair, except that also had other bits of colour in it and looked as though she'd cut it with the kitchen scissors. She wore glasses held together with bits of Sellotape.

I knew where she lived but I didn't want to just knock on the door and start asking questions. You can't tell with parents these days – they can be quite aggressive if they think you're trying to sell them something.

So I waited for her after school, watching all the deaf kids talking with their hands. It reminded me of pigeons taking off. Once she left her group of friends I followed her for a bit and then walked alongside so she could see me and didn't get a fright by not hearing me come up behind her.

She was bigger than me; probably about the same size as Mark, but it was difficult to say how old she was, because the clothes made her look older.

"Hello!" I shouted.

She stopped and took a step back. Maybe I'd shouted too loudly. "Hwa? Who're you?"

"I'm Beanie," I shouted again.

"Stop shou'ing," she said.

She had a bit of a funny voice, I mean, not funny ha ha, but not clear. But I could understand her. "Hwa you wan'?"

"I want to learn signing," I said in my normal voice.

"Clear off," she said and started walking away.

I ran next to her and got a few paces ahead. I realised she'd been looking at my lips when I spoke to her so I made sure she could see my face. "Please," I said, "I've met someone who uses sign language and I want to understand them."

She stopped. "Who?"

"A friend."

"I know all the deaf kids."

"He's not from round here."

She thought about that for a moment. "What kind of signs did he make?"

I showed her the one Malcolm did when I first met him. She looked uncertain. "That means he's hungry."

I had been right!

"And?" she asked.

I showed her the one where Malcolm pulled his hands down the front of the T-shirt with his thumbs near his chest.

She raised her eyebrows. "He's tired," she said. "So who is it tha's hungry and tired?"

I thought I'd better tell her just a little bit more because I needed her cooperation. "His name's Malcolm and he's a new friend of mine."

She looked at me as if to say, "Oh yeah?"

So I answered her. "Honest."

"Who are you?"

"I'm Beanie."

She looked at me as if she was checking me with lie-detector eyes. "That's your nickname."

I nodded. She might have been deaf but she wasn't stupid.

"Have you got any money?" she asked.

"No. I spent it on nuts and raisins for my friend."

She looked as though she didn't believe me again.

"He's a vegetarian," I said.

"A deaf vegetarian. No wonder he's tired and hungry. I can see why he needs help. Come on."

We walked to the local shops where she bought each of us a can of Coke. We sat on a wall just as the sun popped out between the clouds. I took that to be a good sign. I wasn't too sure what else to say. "When in doubt say nowt." That's what Dad always tells me. So, that's what I did. Nothing. Maybe she was thinking or perhaps wasn't too sure what she should say to me. So then the doubt left me and I thought I should show some interest. That always helps break the ice, when you ask questions about other people you've just met. It makes them feel as though you care about them.

"So why are you deaf?" I asked her.

For a minute she didn't say anything and then she said, "I was born deaf."

I thought about that for a moment and didn't really like the thought. Not being able to hear your mum or dad or the telly or singing in class with Mrs Donovan or at the game with Dad... *You'll never walk alone...* imagine not being able to sing for your favourite team. Or listen to music or go to a film or laugh with your mates.

"Hwa?" she said, probably seeing my brain working.

"Nothing."

"You thin' it's terrible being deaf."

I nodded.

"It's all right. I only know being deaf. I have lots of friends. It makes no difference to me what anyone thinks." She swigged her Coke and pointed at my head.

"You wear that all the time?"

"Yes."

"I thought so."

"Are you psychic?"

I took off my beanie.

"Cool," she said, and smiled. "You din't shave it, did you?"

I shook my head.

"Uh huh," she said and looked away as if she wasn't interested but I knew she was.

"I have leukaemia," I told her. "The treatment made my hair fall out."

"Thought so. You're skinny. You don' look too good."

"It'll grow back and I'll gain weight, then I'll be like everyone else."

"Are you going to die?"

"One day. But my grandad was nearly eighty when he died."

"How old are you?"

"Nine years, eleven months and eleven days."

And counting.

Tracy let me walk home with her and I told her as much as I could make up about Malcolm, except of course I didn't tell her where he was or that he was a chimpanzee. All I needed was a book that showed what the signs meant. But I knew Tracy Lewis wasn't going to give me any help without wanting something in return.

"Do you have a lot of friends?" she asked me.

"A few. Not many. I can't play games, not yet anyway. But I'm in a gang. It's my brother's gang. His name is Mark, and there's Rocky, Skimp and Pete-the-Feet."

"Strange names," she said.

"Strange people," I told her.

"I've never been in a gang," Tracy said.

"Well, you're very individual looking, I mean the way you dress, and the colour of your hair, maybe that's why."

"It's because I'm deaf," she said, and then she nodded as if it was a big punctuation mark.

"'No, it's because you're a girl." I thought she should know the truth.

"'I'll teach you to sign," she said and made gestures with her hands. That's exactly what I needed to know how to do. Imagine being able to talk to Malcolm, having a conversation with a monkey, by using my hands. That's called amazing.

"Great," I said.

"But I want to be in your gang."

My heart sank. That was the impossible dream. Like winning the World Cup. Like scoring the final penalty shoot-out. Like running a two-minute mile, or not ever dying.

"It's not my gang," I said, hoping she would just say, "Oh, okay, never mind, I'll teach you anyway."

But she didn't. We got to her house, she opened the gate and closed it and said to me: "That's the deal."

And that's all she said.

9

I am not allowed to call an Extraordinary Meeting of the Executive Council and there was no way that Mark was going to either. He was in the bath when I told him about Tracy, because that's where he is when he comes back from football practice. So I thought that would be the time to explain everything. That way he was less likely to jump out the bath and chase me.

He had soap in his eyes and ears when I first told him what Tracy wanted. He splashed so much water to wash the soap away that it went all over the floor.

Mum has a fit if we make a mess in the bathroom like that, but I thought it wasn't the right moment to remind him.

"No way! What is it with you? I don't care what's going on inside your head, but we're not having a girl in the gang. It's never gonna happen, Jez, get used to the idea and don't mention it again. Now get out!"

I didn't think he would be *that* opposed to the idea. I know there are a couple of girls at school who fancy him, but he plays it very cool and doesn't let on. But I've noticed that when they're around he definitely behaves differently.

"She's twelve and she's very clever. She can talk with her hands. It's called signing. We need it so we can communicate with Malcolm."

"I don't care! Malcolm's a monkey. Monkeys don't talk. They *don't understand*! Understand? Now get out!"

So I did. I had to find a way around this problem. If I went and spoke to Skimp, Pete-the-Feet or Rocky, then that could cause serious complications for the gang. That would undermine the democratic process. It would be as if I was trying to take over. Which of course I can't, because I'm not yet in double figures and even if I was, I wouldn't because Mark is what they call a natural leader.

Sometimes if I get a nosebleed I get some sympathy from Mark, so I closed my eyes and thought hard, imagining the blood coming out my nose and going all over the hall carpet. But nothing happened. Which is just as well, because Mum and Dad always get upset when it does. So how could I get Mark to even think about calling a meeting, never mind considering letting her join?

When he came out the bathroom he walked right past me and slammed his bedroom door in my face before I'd even had a chance to say anything. I pressed my face close to the edge of the door and tapped gently on it. *Tap, tap, tap, tap, tap, tap, tap, tap, tap.* I can keep this up all night and I knew it would wear him down in the end until he'd be forced to open the door.

I'd only done about sixty taps when he yanked open the door. "Stop it! Clear off! I don't want anything to do with you! The subject-matter is closed!"

He was really giving it some welly. Full-in-my-face yelling.

"What's going on up there?" Dad shouts. "Mark! Jez!"

This is where kids who are sick can bend the rules. I whispered to Mark that if he didn't call an EMEC I would tell Mum and Dad that he took me into the Black Gate which is a condemned building, highly dangerous, and could have caused me any number of injuries. And given that Mum and Dad are both scared of me even getting a scratch, because of the risk of infection, they would probably put him up for adoption.

I think there are times Mark would really like to clobber me. I know that this was one of them. His face screwed up into a really angry look, and he grabbed me. In that moment I realised I had pushed him beyond his limits. It must have been all that tapping on the door that had worn down his nerves. Then, something happened to his face, it was as if he had realised he was not going to get the very latest PlayStation for Christmas. He let go of me. And deliberately banged his head against the door two or three times.

Dad called up again: "Mark? What's going on?"

"Nothing," he said.

He went into his room and closed the door without even slamming it.

I knew I had won.

That's called blackmail.

Everyone looked really miserable. Mark kicked his ball again and again against the school wall.

Rocky was twisting fence wire around a piece of wood as if he wanted to strangle it. Skimp seemed to be having a conversation with himself. Every few seconds he'd nod, and then shake his head. He muttered, "I dunno" a couple of times. Pete-the-Feet was nowhere to be seen – he was inside his hair.

"She's more than a girl, she's a deaf girl," Rocky said.

"And she talks funny. Her words don't sound the same as everyone else's," said Pete-the-Feet.

"None of that makes any difference, honest. I talked to her. You just have to listen to what she says. And she dresses really weirdly, so she's interesting," I said encouragingly.

"How can you tell a deaf girl jokes?" Skimp argued.

"It's got nothing to do with her being deaf," Mark said. "This isn't a girl's gang. This is our gang. *My* gang."

He gave the ball a kick that whacked against the wall and would definitely have been a match-winning penalty.

"But we swore an oath to protect Malcolm," I said. This meeting was going nowhere and no one wanted

Tracy Lewis anywhere near them. Except me.

"That's got nothing to do with letting her join us," Pete-the-Feet said, his hair moving from his breath, which at least proved he was alive in there.

"It has everything to do with protecting Malcolm. She can find out what he's trying to say. He might hold really vital information. And imagine that, we would be the ones who discovered it *because* you let Tracy Lewis join in." I said "you" rather than "we" because that kept me, the probation gang member, out of it. It made them feel more important.

"She could be an associate member," Skimp suggested. "Or even a consultant."

"A what?" Rocky said, giving the helpless stick a final, deadly twist.

"Skimp's right," I said. "That's exactly what she'd be – a consultant. She's an expert in something and we need her services. She could be an associate member while she's a consultant, and then when she's told us what Malcolm's trying to tell us, we could tell her her services are no longer required," I urged them. After all, I had to go along with them on this whole "girl" thing. Personally, I figured that once Tracy had spent all of sixty seconds in our company she would rather move into a zoo with Malcolm.

"But what about the jokes?" Rocky said.

"All you have to do is make sure she can see your lips," I said, trying to make things easier for Tracy's membership. "She's got a great sense of humour."

"How would you know?" Mark said all miserable-like, still irritated because everything was my fault.

"Because she wants to join the gang. How funny is that?"

The realisation crept over them like a measles rash. Skimp smiled. Rocky grunted and Pete-the-Feet actually chuckled.

"Beanie's right, she must have a twisted sense of humour, wanting to join an all-boy gang," Rocky conceded.

Mission accomplished.

I gave my next forged letter to Mrs Carpenter who was teaching Science – and I thought she might have been relieved when I gave it to her because her class was about micro-organisms which can cause illness and viruses that can… well, I didn't really need to sit in *that* class, did I?

The gang had done a really good job of collecting

food for Malcolm and my backpack was full of fruit. When I squeezed through the gate I still went very carefully round the track, just in case anyone else was hanging around. But as usual, the haunted house kept everyone else away. I waited till I got to the foot of the stairs, but then, before I could even call out his name, I heard him running along the upstairs corridor and bounding down the stairs.

He must have been watching from his window and had recognised me, which made me feel really nice inside. He was only about the size of a little three or four year old, but when he jumped up on me he was very heavy and I fell over. He was all over me like a bouncy toy and I was laughing so much I couldn't get up.

I made the "I am hungry" sign and he opened his mouth and stuck his fingers inside. It was time for a picnic.

I got onto the sacks in the greenhouse and opened up all the food. We sat together, peeled bananas and got through the recommended five pieces of fruit. Over the last couple of visits Malcolm and I had developed a little routine. We would greet each other and then eat something and then he would take my hand and lead me on a tour of the house. We'd go into every room and I would imagine who must have lived there, because in its day it must have been a very beautiful house. But you could see the big cracks up the wall and the bits of ceiling that had fallen down and the holes in the roof where the birds came in and made their nests in the rafters, and in a way it made me feel quite sad that it was falling down. But on the other hand the birds and Malcolm had found a home. And, as Mark always says, we all aspire to better things in life. So I suppose Malcolm and the birds have gone up in the world.

After our tour we would go back to the greenhouse and snuggle down into the sacks and have a nap. But today we stayed up in the bedroom and looked out the window because I knew Mark and the gang had gone to get Tracy. I saw someone creeping through the bushes and almost banged on the window to tell them where I was. But then I saw it was two men – it was Potato Face and Comb Head! And they were going around the house, checking to see if they could get inside.

When we had decided to protect Malcolm, Rocky and Skimp had pulled the old kitchen door back into place and put all sorts of rubbish in front of it as a deterrent to anyone else getting in. Then we had found a small hole in the wall at the back courtyard, and that's where we all squeezed through now.

Malcolm's teeth chattered. I held him as we watched the men give up trying to get in the house. I realised that sooner or later someone who wouldn't care that the Black Gate was haunted was going to break in. And when they did that they might not realise that the reason Malcolm made all those threatening noises was because he was scared. Then they might get the wrong idea and try and hurt him. I had done my research on Mark's computer and when we first thought that Malcolm was grinning and being happy it really meant he was distressed and frightened. Things aren't always what they seem.

It wasn't long before Mark and the others arrived.

"Potato Face and Comb Head were here," I told them.

"Did they get in?" Mark asked.

"No. But they might come back."

"I'll set some booby traps before we go," Rocky said.

"Yeah, well don't forget to tell us where!" Skimp told him.

"Remember, we've got a girl to worry about now," Mark said.

I looked at Tracy – had she heard?

"They don't want me in the gang, do they?" she said to me.

I shook my head. "Did they say anything insulting when they went to get you?" I asked.

"If they did I didn't hear them," she said and then smiled. Told you. Great sense of humour.

She didn't seem to care much about Mark and the others, she just looked at the size of the old house and said, "Wow." Everyone else just stood there. I don't think that we were used to the idea yet of a girl being with us. "Where is he?" she asked.

"You have to sit down and be quiet," Mark told her as I called Malcolm, who hid in the bushes until he felt safe to come out. I could tell everyone was waiting to see just what Tracy was going to do with him.

Tracy's eyes widened. Her jaw dropped. She said, "Wow" again. And then she smiled. That's what Malcolm does to you. He makes you feel good.

Malcolm wasn't too sure about the new member

of the gang. And he clung to my legs until I eased his hand free and sat down with him. Then Tracy started talking with her hands. Malcolm looked at me, rubbed his face with his hands and looked again – as if in disbelief that someone else was talking like that.

"He doesn't know much," Tracy said. "Only some very basic stuff." She used her hands again and this time Malcolm responded. He touched his chest and then his lips and then me.

"He says he loves you, Beanie."

No one said anything, but I could tell that the others were quietly fascinated by Tracy, even though she spoke slowly and with some difficulty. Me? I just felt very special after what Malcolm had said. Tracy kept making gestures.

"He knows a few things, like when he's scared or tired and enough to ask for food and to say when something hurts him or when he feels sick," she said.

I stroked his head and he wrapped his arms around me and Skimp gave him some chewing gum. Then we all sat around and chewed and blew bubbles. Malcolm was getting quite good at it and had less in his fur this time.

"Why would they teach him those things?" Skimp asked.

Mark said, "It must have something to do with that hospital tag on his wrist."

I looked at my own plastic bracelet on my wrist that the hospital gave me. It had my name and my date of birth, but Malcolm's was all worn. Then I thought that as I go into hospital and have treatment, maybe it was the same for him. "What if he was in an animal hospital and escaped?" I said. "What if he's really sick and needs treatment?"

"Maybe it wasn't a hospital he escaped from," said Mark. "What if he ran away from a laboratory where they experiment on animals?"

I suddenly felt sick. Even sicker than when I go for treatment.

Tracy used her hands again. But then she shook her head. "He doesn't understand that question, so he's only got a very limited vocabulary and response."

Then Rocky said something really scary. "There's a military biological research centre about thirty miles from here. You know, just past the cooling towers – all those buildings there, that's why they've got a private road and guards at the gates. My uncle told me that's where they do experiments on germ warfare and stuff."

Was Malcolm being experimented on? That sounded like torture. No one said anything for a few seconds, but then Malcolm squealed and started to panic. I grabbed him and held him. Mark jumped to his feet. "Quiet everyone! Listen!"

Tracy looked at me because obviously she hadn't heard him and I just put a finger to my lips and gestured for her to stay where she was.

"Dogs!" Rocky said.

Mark ran from the greenhouse into the kitchen and I could just see him peeping through the crack with the boards covered the windows. Then he came back in a hurry. "It's the police with a dog unit," he hissed.

"Get your bag, Beanie!" Rocky said, and started throwing the scraps of fruit away into the bushes.

"We'll have to make a run for it," said Mark. "Those dogs will smell us and Malcolm, and the cops will find the way we came in."

Tracy was watching Rocky and Mark as they whispered orders.

"I'll make a run for it, and draw them away,"

Pete-the-Feet said, pulling his hair back and tying it with an elastic band. He was ready to run. "Then you get going with Malcolm."

Tracy waved her hand at them. "No," she said, "I'll stay. It will take them ages to question me. I can keep them busy for a long time."

She went closer to Malcolm and made a couple of signs. "I told him he has to stay quiet and go with you," she said to us all. She stroked Malcolm's head, and made a sign with her hand, and mouthed carefully, "Understand?"

Malcolm climbed onto my back and held on tightly.

"Can you carry him?" asked Mark.

"I'll manage," I told him as Rocky grabbed my backpack and pulled it on his chest because he was also carrying his own school pack full of books.

"I'll take point," he said, and headed for the hole in the wall. We could hear the dogs barking now. They were close.

"Come on, Beanie," Skimp said. "Hurry."

I looked at Tracy and make sure she could see what I was saying. "Thank you," I said. Mark pulled me away.

Then we left her. All alone. She was our rear-guard defence, Rocky said as he made a pointed gesture at her. Ace. Good stuff. Respect.

In that moment of self-sacrifice Tracy Lewis, a deaf kid who dressed like a charity shop princess, became my heroine.

10

We ran down the track towards the gate, and when we got there Mark pulled Malcolm off my back so I could squeeze through. But he made such a noise, because he was so scared, that we had to push him through quickly so he could climb back onto my shoulder. The police car that stood at the gates was empty, the cops had already moved around the back of the house, but we could still hear the dogs barking frantically.

"I hope Tracy will be okay," Skimp said.

"She'll be fine," Mark told him. "She'll have them tied up in knots. Come on, run!"

Malcolm might have only been the size of a small three or four year old but he was heavy and I could feel the sweat making my shirt stick. My head was baking so I shoved my beanie into my pocket and let the cold air cool me down.

Rocky was way ahead, making sure the streets

and the back alleys that we used to get home were clear. But after about five minutes I was so tired I could have gone to sleep while I was still running.

"Hang on!" Mark shouted at the others.

I had to sit down. I was shaking and felt sick. Malcolm was holding on so tightly I could barely breathe. He looked at me and I made the sign that he had shown me when he was tired in the house. That seemed to work and he relaxed a bit and cuddled up to me.

I had my back against the wall and while Mark loosened my anorak Pete-the-Feet gave me some water. That made me feel a lot better, but I wished I had a banana for some energy.

"You've got to let one of us carry Malcolm," Mark said.

"No!" I cried. "You'll frighten him."

Pete-the-Feet was already stroking Malcolm's head, and Malcolm was holding his hand like he was a frightened child. "I think he'll be okay with me," said Pete-the-Feet.

I looked at Malcolm. He seemed quite confused, and I was worried he would just run away and get lost in the housing estate. Then the dogs would chase him and people would be phoning the police and the next thing he knew he'd be back being experimented on.

"I'll be all right in a minute," I said, catching my breath.

"No you won't," Mark said, "but we're gonna go a bit slower now, and Pete-the-Feet can take Malcolm, and you can walk next to him and hold his hand. How does that sound?"

Sometimes you just have to do as you're told, so I said yes, that would be okay. Pete-the-Feet carefully lifted Malcolm and let him wrap his arms around his chest. I got up and stood next to him. I was too short for Malcolm's arm to reach down and hold my hand, but his foot came out and gripped it, so that was okay. We could still hang on to each other.

Rocky did a good job of getting us to Pete-the-Feet's house without anyone spotting us. We piled into the kitchen and Skimp and Rocky raided the fridge. There were chocolate biscuits and milk and we all sat around the big old pine table and just scoffed. I felt a bit better then. And Malcolm was sitting next to me and he had a milk moustache which we all thought was really funny. And we laughed like broken drains, but I think that was just the release of tension, because we had all been scared. Scared and worried that Malcolm was going to be taken away from us. Because I think everybody loved Malcolm by then.

"We've got to find a place to hide him," Rocky said.

"He can't stay here, because we've only got two bedrooms and my mum's likely to turn him in for the reward money," Pete-the-Feet said.

"There's a reward for Malcolm?" Skimp asked.

"There's bound to be, isn't there? That's why the cops were out hunting him with the dogs, like an escaped convict," said Rocky.

"We don't know that," said Mark, "but Rocky's right. We have to find somewhere safe for Malcolm until we decide what to do with him."

"We're not going to do anything with him!" I said. "He's going to live with us."

"Yeah, right," Mark said sarcastically.

"We've got to take him *somewhere*. Everybody's going to be coming home from work soon, so it's not gonna be easy walking down the street with him. Someone will see him and then it's all over," Rocky said.

"My dad's got an old touring caravan in a lock-up on the industrial estate." Skimp said. "He'd be safe in there. I just have to find the keys."

"That's a great idea. But how do we get him out of here without anyone spotting him?" said Mark.

"My sister's got an old pushchair in the shed. It's one of those things with a plastic rain cover. We could strap Malcolm in there. He's already got Beanie's T-shirt on and providing nobody looked too closely we could get away with it, don't you think?" Pete-the-Feet said.

I think Mark knew that I was getting a bit scared for Malcolm. He turned to me and said, "What do you think, Jez?"

Which was really very considerate of him, considering he's my older brother and often says I cause him grief.

Malcolm had biscuit crumbs all over his face and was still guzzling milk. He was a messy child, as Mum would say. "I don't want to leave him," I said. "I don't want him to be lost and frightened. I want him to come home with me."

"Listen, Jez, you've got to go for your treatment tomorrow, so he'll have to be on his own anyway.

I think it's better we get him into the caravan. He'll be safe there," Mark told me as he gave Malcolm another chocolate digestive – which was doing a good job of keeping him quiet.

"I can't get the keys until tomorrow," Skimp said.

Mark thought for a moment. "OK. This is what we'll do. We'll take Malcolm to our house and hide him in Jez's room for tonight. Then, when Jez goes to the hospital, the rest of us will bunk school and get him into the caravan."

Everyone was nodding, including me, because at least I had another twelve hours to think of a better way of hiding and looking after Malcolm.

Pete-the-Feet was right. If you didn't look too closely you could almost think that Malcolm was a small child. We strapped him into the pushchair and Rocky pulled Pete-the-Feet's mum's knitted tea cosy over Malcolm's head so his ears stuck out each hole. By the time we had zipped him in beneath the plastic and given him a banana to chew on we were all set.

It was quite nerve-wracking, because we had to pass people carrying their shopping, others getting off buses, some going across traffic lights, and then it started raining and we were worried that the rain splattering on the plastic cover would scare Malcolm.

But we were almost home. Almost.

"Oh no," Pete-the-Feet groaned. "It's Mrs Blanchard from number eighty-six. She's the nosiest woman in the street."

We saw a woman who had a leather jacket on and clumpy boots and who was as old as Gran. Mum would have said it was mutton dressed up as lamb. That's called a metaphor.

She was smoking a soggy-looking cigarette.

Pete-the-Feet muttered: "She's really suspicious. She'll probably think we're child kidnappers or something. She's been down the bingo hall and she usually goes for a drink in the pub afterwards – so that might save us. Don't say anything unless you really have to. Talk about the weather or something if she stops us."

"Hello, Peter, where are you off to, then, down this end of town?" Mrs Blanchard said as we all reached the same crack in the pavement.

We just looked at her as we stood in the drizzle, hoping that one of us would think of something quick to say. We didn't.

"Blimey, I've never seen lads as quiet as you lot. That usually means you've been up to something, eh?"

We must have looked like a bunch of convicts caught on the run, because then she laughed. "Oh, get you lot! Come on! Give your face a holiday. Smile! I was only kidding."

And then without taking a breath she bent down and peered into the pram.

"Who's this then?" she said, wiping the rain off the plastic. Thankfully, the old crinkled and yellowed plastic blurred Malcolm. But she kept looking.

"It's my auntie Joan's baby," I said.

"And who are you when you're at home?" she said, squinting at me.

"My name is Beanie and this is my mum's sister's baby and we're taking him home because she had to go out shopping so she paid us to babysit him."

"Beanie? What sort of name is that?" She peered back into the plastic. "Well, it's lovely that your auntie Joan trusts you with her baby. How old is he?"

"Three," I said at exactly the same time as Mark said, "Four," and Pete-the-Feet said, "Don't know."

"He's *nearly* four," I said quickly.

"Oh." She bent down again. I could only imagine

what Malcolm must be seeing as the moon-faced Mrs Blanchard with her wobbly jowls pushed her nose close to the pushchair. It must have looked like a soggy balloon with a face drawn on it. Please don't do your monkey scream, I begged him in my head.

"It's a bit unusual for a child of that age to have so much hair," she said.

"He's wearing a fleece," I told her. "He's a very beautiful three year old."

"Oh. Well, I'm sure he is. I haven't got my glasses. Hang on a bit." She started rummaging in her handbag. "I've got them here."

"Sorry, Mrs Blanchard, we've got to run. There's our bus. We've got to get Malcolm home for his tea," Pete-the-Feet said, and pushed the pram away, with the rest of us following.

She didn't really have much of a chance to say anything else other than, "Well, Malcolm's a nice name anyway."

Which I was pleased about because it meant I had chosen the right name for him.

We pushed him past a row of shops and then down Cavendish Road, which meant we had gone in almost a big circle to keep us off the streets where people might know us. Just as we had one more street to go a police car came around the corner. They were driving so slowly you just knew they were looking for someone.

They stopped.

"All right, lads? What are you lot up to then?"

"Just walking," Skimp said.

"Walking where?" the cop said.

"Down there," said Rocky.

"Down where?" said the cop.

"Meeting his mum," Mark said, pointing to Skimp.

"We're looking for a monkey," said the cop.

"He's sitting next to you," Pete-the-Feet said.

The driver leaned across his mate and pointed a finger. "Don't get cheeky with me, son."

The first cop smiled. "Small monkey. A young chimpanzee. It's gone missing," he said.

"It sounds like Auntie Joan's toddler," I said. "He's in the pushchair. Do you want to see him?"

"You kids are something cruel, you are," the policeman said.

Then they drove off.

This time "almost" became "definitely". We were at our house.

I could see Dad was in his shed. I think he was trying to make Mum a footstool because she always says how tired she is at night. He's been making it for a while now, but the legs are always a different length and so the stool is always wonky. It's her birthday soon, so I think he'll probably give up any day now and go down to B&Q and buy a flat pack one.

The good thing is that it keeps him busy. While everybody else went into the house and took Malcolm out the pushchair and up to my room I went in and said hello to Dad.

He had just lifted the footstool off the bench onto the floor but you could see right away that it just wasn't going to work. Wonky is the only word you could use for it.

I told him I'd been out with Mark and that now I was going to have something to eat and do a bit of homework. He was nodding, listening to me, but with his attention focused on the footstool. Then he looked at me, and for a second I thought he could see all the lies I was storing in my head.

"You're home late."

"I went round to Skimp's with Rocky and Pete-the-Feet and Mark and…" I almost said Malcolm, and that could have opened up a whole new line of questioning.

"I didn't know it was so late," he said. "I'd better go and collect Mum."

That would keep him out the house for a least an hour, because he always goes early to collect her from the supermarket and he ends up on the magazine and DVD shelves. I think Dad does most of his reading in Sainsbury's.

Back in the house everyone was very quiet. "Where's Malcolm?" I asked.

"Shush, Jez, he's sleeping," Mark said.

I pulled off my coat and ran upstairs.

The good thing about having an older brother is that when you move to a new house, as we did a couple of years ago, they get their own room. Which means I got my own room, which is better than sharing. So I still had the bunk beds in my room.

I usually just put my clothes on the top bunk and sleep on the bottom. It's much easier than having to open and close the wardrobe or the drawers. You just fall out of bed, reach up and grab your shirt and underpants and that's it. Just like Clark Kent.

Pete-the-Feet, because he's so tall, had been able to reach up and lie Malcolm down on the top bunk without disturbing him. The little chimpanzee was fast asleep; it must have been all the fear and tension and excitement of what had happened at the Black Gate. I knew how he felt.

They had covered him up with my duvet and put my old teddy bear next to him to keep him warm. It's not really my teddy bear, it's Mark's, but he's too cool to admit that now. So the teddy bear just lives on the top bunk, usually with my undies thrown on top of his head.

I stepped up and put my face next to Malcolm's. He was Harry Gonkers, which Rocky's uncle told him was army slang for being fast asleep.

Mark came upstairs and we whispered. "Where's everyone?" I said.

"Gone home. Rocky's going round to Tracy's to see she's all right."

"We might have been sunk without her," I said.

Mark shrugged. He knows girls can do tough stuff – we've all watched *Spooks*. It's just a bit different when they're in your gang.

"I'm going to stay here in case he wakes up," I said.

"It'll be a problem when he does."

"I know."

"What are we going to do?"

"I'll think of something," I said.

"Like what?"

"I don't know. I haven't thought of it yet, have I?"

Malcolm might be dead to the world right now, but if he woke up and started swinging from the light bulb, we were all going to be in trouble.

"We've got to keep him amused somehow," Mark said. "Blimey, Jez, you don't half cause problems."

"I know. I'm sorry, Mark. I didn't want anyone else to get involved. But I'm glad you are. I couldn't have managed on my own." And I meant it. My brother had been really good, had accepted Malcolm and made the gang his bodyguard. You couldn't ask much more from a brother, could you?

"Yeah, well." He shrugged again. Shrugging is what he does. It means a lot of things. Quite often it means, *Don't embarrass me by saying something soppy*. So I knew everything was all right between us. But neither of us knew how we were going to get through till tomorrow, when the gang could take Malcolm and hide him in the caravan.

"Anyway, we'll have to think of something," he said. "We could always tell them he's a long-lost relative."

Which in a way is true.

I climbed up and snuggled down next to my sleeping friend. He still smelled warm and furry, and a bit doggish. And I could imagine us sleeping together in the tree tops in the special nests that chimpanzees make.

We would lie there and let the wind gently rock the tree. If it rained we could hold a big banana leaf over our heads and just sit there and reach up and touch the clouds.

I always get butterflies in my stomach when I go to the hospital for treatment. Everyone is very nice there and they're very kind to me, but it's still hospital. And it is still treatment. But it's really important for me to do it, so there's not much use complaining about it. I think it's worse for Mum and Dad sometimes. It depends how they are, because when we have our tea the night before and we're all sitting around with the telly on in the background and we're oohing and aahing about this and that – and Mum's telling Mark not to talk with his mouth full, and Dad is laughing at something really unfunny on the telly, then sometimes they get a bit too boisterous. I mean, you can see they're not *really* laughing. They're hiding.

Mum brings home organic everything. She says it's better for me and will help my immune system. I wallop down the broccoli first and then get into the roast potatoes and gravy.

But tonight, they seemed to be laughing a lot.

"I'm going upstairs," I said and they gave each other a funny look which meant, *Is he all right? What's wrong with him? You think he's feeling sick? You think it's about tomorrow?* And anything else you can think of that might be worrying them about me.

"I'm all right," I said. "I've just got a project I'm working on, and Mark said he would help me because he's going to lend me his computer."

Mark opened his mouth and you could see half the sausage still in there. "I did not!"

"Mark! Don't talk with your mouth full of food," Dad said, even though he was chewing a potato at the time. It's a different world being a grown-up.

"Yes, you did, don't you remember? We were going to research monkeys."

Mark had no choice. He swallowed. "Oh yeah, I remember."

"What about your pud?" Dad said. "You're not going to miss your favourite, are you?"

There was custard and chopped banana for pudding.

"Can I take it up with me? I want to start on the project."

"I suppose," said Mum.

"Can I have some extra bananas as well?"

"Extra?"

"In case I wake up in the night and want a snack."

"Do you normally wake up in the night and want a snack?" Mum asked.

"Quite often. I sometimes come downstairs and mooch around."

"That's the first I've heard of it," Dad said.

"You never hear me because I'm very quiet. And you're always snoring anyway."

They looked at each other. Mum shrugged. "That's true, Jim. You do snore a lot."

"Do I?"

"Always."

"I didn't know that. You've never said."

Mum absentmindedly gave me a couple of extra bananas with one already chopped into the custard. They were just talking away between themselves. The only thing she said as I went out the door was: "Don't make a mess."

I sometimes find their expectations a bit unrealistic.

I'm nine years, eleven months and twelve days old. I'm supposed to make a mess.

Mark brought his laptop into my room. "You could have warned me," he said. "Under any other circumstances I wouldn't let you near my computer."

"I know, but I had a brainwave when I was eating the broccoli – maybe it really is brain food after all – so I thought that if we had a project with chimpanzees on the screen and Malcolm woke up, then that would cover any noises he made."

I think Mark realised then that I was the one with the brains in our family. If ever he made Prime Minister because of his leadership skills I would have to be the one pulling the strings behind the scenes.

Malcolm was sitting under the duvet that we had draped like a tent across the edge of my bed and a chair, the tea cosy still on his head. I didn't want his brain to get too hot, because that's what tea cosies do, they keep teapots warm. I pointed and pulled off my beanie. He copied me and rubbed his head.

He was looking around at his new surroundings. He spent a lot of time gazing at the poster of Steven Gerrard on the wall, and then he looked at the T-shirt I'd given him.

I'm sure he made the connection.

I spooned some custard into his mouth but he spat it out and it made an interesting pattern on the wall. I think it must have been too hot. I blew on it, and he soon ate both mine and Mark's. That was quite a sacrifice. Custard and sliced bananas is an age-old favourite in our house.

Mark and I set up the laptop so that I could sit on the top bunk and have it open, so that if Mum or Dad came in I might be able to hide Malcolm quickly. That's when we made a bit of a mistake. As soon as he saw video links of chimpanzees in the wild he went nuts. He screamed and chattered and had a right old fit. He chucked the bedding everywhere.

Dad called up the stairs: "Mark! Jez! Turn that thing down, will you?"

But Malcolm was in full frenzy. Mark turned the picture off the screen and I made a grab for Malcolm, who was trying to reach the light. If he leapt onto that the whole ceiling would come down.

Dad was halfway up the stairs.

"Lads! Did you hear what I said?"

Mark had hold of Malcolm's feet and I wrestled him under the bedclothes and shoved a half-peeled banana into his mouth, then put a finger to my lips – which was a sign that anyone could understand. Malcolm sucked and chewed the banana, turning it into a gooey pulp. He took some of it out of his mouth and examined it, then sucked it off his finger.

He would fit in nicely at the school canteen.

After half an hour Mark went downstairs to make Malcolm some hot chocolate. We thought this would help make him sleep through the night. Malcolm sat on the bunk reading comics while I tried to do some more research on how to look after chimpanzees who were on the run.

The round face of a chimpanzee stared at me

from the screen. It wasn't as beautiful as Malcolm but it had that same appealing look. Did I know, the text on the screen asked me, that chimpanzees have ninety-eight per cent of the same genes as us?

"I didn't know that," I told the computer. That's amazing! Malcolm and me are nearly the same people. There's only two per cent between us. That's like semi-skimmed and full-cream milk. There's virtually no difference. One's slightly fattier than the other is all! I looked at Malcolm, who had a quizzical look on his face as he studied the amazing artwork in *Silver Surfer*, and it made the whole idea of someone experimenting on him even more horrible.

I felt very fuzzy inside as I looked at him reading my comic upside down; he was so close to getting it right.

Mark came back with his sports-drink bottle full of warm milk. "I thought he could suck through this without making a mess," he said. Then he looked at me. "What's up?"

"Malcolm is nearly one of us," I said.

"Well, his eating habits certainly qualify him."

I suddenly felt a bit tearful. I don't know why, it just started to come out. Mark's face screwed up because I don't think he knew what to do. "What?" he asked.

I wiped the tears away with my pyjama sleeve. "Nothing."

"It'll be all right, Jez," he said and touched my arm. "Mum and Dad will be with you tomorrow."

I wasn't upset about that. I was thinking about Malcolm, the small lost chimpanzee being chased by someone. He had no home, he'd been separated from his family, and someone wanted to lock him up in a cage and hurt him.

And there was only me to hold his hand and tell him it'd be all right. Just like Mum and Dad did with me.

But I wasn't sure that it was going to be all right.

If Rocky had been sleeping over he'd have lain in the corridor guarding our bedroom door, because he'd have thought he was "on stag". Which is what soldiers call doing guard duty. Rocky knows all those things, but it would have been a bit difficult explaining to Mum and Dad that Rocky was "on stag" because we had an escaped chimpanzee sleeping in my top bunk. So we decided that I would sleep on top and cover Malcolm and me with the duvet and that Mark would sleep on the bottom bunk.

We hid Malcolm in Mark's room and told Mum and Dad that I was feeling a bit iffy about tomorrow so Mark wanted to stay in my room with me. You could tell they thought this was Mark being really sweet and very kind towards his younger brother. Which I suppose was true in a way.

Mum came in and tucked me up. She crinkled her nose a bit and said she'd better wash the duvet cover again – it smelled a bit doggy – while Dad said I should change my socks more often. Once we heard them go to bed and the toilet flush and the light go out beneath their door, we went into Mark's room and carried Malcolm back. He was very dopey.

"The hot milk worked a treat," I whispered.

"It wasn't the hot milk, it was one of Mum's Valium pills I put in it. I nicked it out her handbag when I went downstairs."

"You drugged Malcolm? You could kill him!" I hissed.

"No, I won't. It's only a mild sedative to stop Mum from cracking up."

Those 'circumstances' again. I checked Malcolm's

breathing. It was slow but regular. Mark pulled the mattress on the floor blocking the door just in case Mum or Dad came in, which would give us a chance to make sure Malcolm was hidden under the bedclothes. I snuggled down next to Malcolm.

I knew I wouldn't sleep a wink. Tomorrow was a big day in more ways than one. Malcolm was going to be smuggled out like a prisoner of war, and then we had to think of how I could get him back to Africa, where he could sit in those tall trees and shelter under banana leaves and find a chimpanzee family to adopt him. Maybe one day he would teach them sign language and tell them about his big adventure where he came across other chimpanzees, but who had much less fur. I imagined the breeze ruffling the high branches, and felt it gently rocking the monkeys to sleep.

Me too.

11

When it's hospital day I am always up first. We have to get there early and Mum usually has only a quick cup of tea before we leave. I don't get to eat anything. I usually moan and groan, but this morning I was glad to get out the house and leave Mark to look after Malcolm.

"Don't forget to take him to the loo. He'll need a pee," I told Mark.

"Chimpanzees don't use toilets," he said.

"Well, he's got to go somewhere," I told him. "And as soon as Mum and me leave, get Malcolm to the caravan."

He nodded.

"And give him some breakfast. Coco Pops or something. And toast."

I showed Malcolm the palm of my hand held up. I hoped he would understand that I wanted him to stay here. Then I put a finger to my lips again.

He just sat down and looked at me. Talking with your hands is really difficult, so all I could do was touch my chest and my lips to show him I loved him.

Then I gave him my Rubik's cube to play with.

They make a real effort at our hospital to help sick children feel as comfortable as possible. That's what they told me when I first went there. The being comfortable bit wasn't exactly true because of the treatment, but you get used to it and now when I lie on the bed I look at all the different colours they painted the walls.

Apparently, the combination of the colours orange and blue has a calming effect and the room I was in had these two colours going around it with quite jolly paintings of cartoon characters. It feels a bit like being in the middle of *Toy Story* or *Shrek*. I prefer to have Mum wait outside because it can't be very pleasant for her seeing me get treatment. And besides, sometimes I can't help it and I cry, just a bit, and I don't want her seeing that. I sometimes feel a bit sorry for myself, but then I think of Dad pushing that huge trolley full of letters and I have to tell myself that I'm very lucky that I don't have to do that as well.

Dr Mansfield had a new trainee doctor with her. At least I think he was a trainee, because he watched what she did very carefully. She let him have a go and he seemed to be all right. His name was Dr Morgan, but he says I can call him Rick. I tell him he can call me Beanie. It's probably better to be a bit personal when someone's sticking needles into you.

Dr Mansfield is a nice lady doctor and she is the one who looks after me when I go for my treatment.

"Are you all right, Beanie?" she asked me. "You seem a bit unhappy today. Not that being here is anything to be pleased about, is it?"

"I'm all right. Did you hear about me trying to save the Sweet Dreams Sweet Factory?"

"I didn't, no. Why does it need saving?"

"Mum used to work there and I haven't had any Tube Sucks since they closed down. It was also going to be a secret headquarters for the gang I'm in."

"That's very interesting," she said. But it wasn't, not to her; she was just being polite as she fiddled with the equipment and checked my chart, while Rick took my pulse with one of those little clothes-peg thermometers that you stick on the end of your finger. Then he put another thermometer in my ear.

"Nothing in there that I can see," he said and grinned.

"Are you saying I've got no brain?" I said with a straight face.

He looked as though he'd sat on one of his own needles. "No, no... I was just..."

I laughed. And he knew I was teasing. That's the trouble these days, you can't say anything that might offend anyone, even if you're just kidding. Dad says that if you can't have fun poked at you then you're going to grow up a really miserable so-and-so. Anyway, it was an old joke. Dad did one much better when I had an ear infection. He looked in with his big torch and blew in my ear. The next thing I knew there was a feather in my other ear. "Head full of feathers," he said. I still don't know how he got the feather in there.

"Your temperature's up a bit," Rick said. He picked my beanie up off the chair and looked at it. "This must keep the heat in, like a tea cosy on a teapot."

And of course that made me think even more about Malcolm. I was really worried that they weren't going to get him into the caravan and that the police and the RSPCA were going to catch him.

Dr Mansfield watched me and I could see she knew something was bothering me – and it wasn't just the Sweet Dreams Sweet Factory. That's called perception.

I had to tell them something otherwise they would scribble notes on that clipboard about me being upset, or that the treatment wasn't working properly, or that they were going to give me something else, or that...

"I was doing a school project on chimpanzees," I told them. "Did you know there's only two per cent difference in the genes between them and us?"

"I did know that, actually," Dr Mansfield said. "They're what's called sentient beings."

That was a new word I hadn't heard before, but it sounded quite important in relation to Malcolm. "What does that mean?"

"Well, it means they have a consciousness, like you and me. They can experience emotions," she said.

"Like being frightened?" I asked her.

"Oh yes. Many animals can sense and experience fear."

"And what about feelings? I mean, could they

feel the same as I do about Mum and Dad?"

"Yes, I believe so. Primates are raised in family groups."

"So they'd miss *their* mum and dad if they were separated from them?"

"I suppose they would."

"And they would need someone else to love them and look after them? Because otherwise they could just be sad and lonely."

"I suppose so."

I was feeling sick by now, though that's not unusual when I come for treatment, but I think this was like before, when I thought of Malcolm being alone and scared. Whatever feelings I had for him must be pretty big on the sentient scale of things.

"So it's pretty horrible when you think that people capture chimpanzees and other monkeys and put them in cages and then take them into laboratories and do tests on them. If someone did that to me I'd be terrified. It's bad enough coming in here for treatment, where people are nice to me and explain things about what they're going to do. It's not very pleasant and it hurts sometimes, but at least I understand."

"Is that what you've read in your project?"

I nodded.

"Well," she said very gently, "not all experiments and research are done on animals these days. Scientists often use live tissue culture instead."

Dr Rick was doing something to the monitor screen that showed the levels of stuff they were putting into me and said, "Yes, but if it wasn't for animal experiments there'd be no cancer research, no nothing research. You try telling someone really sick that they can't get cured because someone doesn't want to test a new drug on an animal."

Sometimes you can see what people are thinking when you look at their face. Dr Mansfield's expression didn't change that much, but there was a sort of different light in her eyes.

"I don't think this is the place to discuss that, do you?" she said.

Dr Rick shrugged, and started to say: "Look, all I'm saying is that if there are no experiments..." He stopped because he realised Dr Mansfield must have been warning him with that look. He glanced at me, and then lowered his eyes. I could tell he was embarrassed. "I'd better just go and check some stuff outside," he said and left the room.

I think Dr Mansfield would like to have said a lot more. I think she was kind enough that she would have wanted to tell me that someone like Malcolm had not been harmed in order for me to get better. But she just gave one of those encouraging smiles and made sure the tube was taped properly to my arm. "There," she said, "won't be long now. You'll soon be home."

It couldn't be soon enough. I knew now more than ever that I had to save Malcolm from getting hurt.

Dad always comes to the hospital and he's the one who thinks of a joke afterwards. Mum laughs too, but she doesn't do the cracking-up laugh that Dad gets before he even finishes the joke. It drives everyone crazy. He's almost there, almost at the end of the joke and he's in fits. He laughs so much that I always start laughing with him. The tears roll down his face and I'm creased up because I can't help it. He's snorting like a donkey, Mum is trying to drive and I'm screaming for him to tell me the end of the joke. When he eventually gets there it's usually a rubbish joke. I don't know what he thought was so funny to start with – but you have to laugh.

I usually lie flat out on the sofa after I've had my treatment. I feel rotten – but not as rubbish I'd feel if Dad hadn't done his daft act. Sometimes I throw up, sometimes I don't.

"Jez? Use the downstairs loo," Mum called after me.

"No, I'm all right!" I shouted back as I went upstairs. I felt awful, and I knew I was going to puke sooner or later, but I had to see if Malcolm was still in the house. My room looked as though a hurricane had hit it.

Mark was sitting in front of the wardrobe and put a finger to his lips.

"What?" I whispered.

"We couldn't get Malcolm to come with us to the caravan. He went bananas. I managed to corner him and get him into the wardrobe," Mark said.

"You've trapped him? He'll be terrified," I told him as I got down on my hands and knees and pulled him out the way.

Mark grabbed hold of me. "Listen, if he'd have got out the room he would have been gone for ever. I had to get him in there."

I squeezed the door open a bit and put my face in the crack. "Whoo whoo," I whispered. "Malcolm, it's me – Beanie. Don't be frightened."

A hairy finger came out the wardrobe and touched my nose. The door burst open and Mark and me fell backwards. Malcolm was all over me, screeching and howling.

"Shut him up!" Mark hissed.

I tried. But you know how it is when you have an excited chimpanzee running around your room.

When you're sick and go to our hospital they always give you a handful of sweets to suck. I pulled a lollipop out and gave it to Malcolm. The quickest way to keep a child quiet is to give it a sweet. I've heard Mum's friend, Mrs Wallace, tell her that, and she should know – she's got four – but Mum doesn't agree with that, I've heard her say it's too much sugar. I think Mum is wrong. Malcolm sucked the sweet like it was the last thing he'd ever eat.

I was just about to pick him up and put him back into bed when the doorbell rang.

Mark and I froze. No one comes to our house during the day except the man to read the electricity meter and he was here last week. There were muffled voices downstairs.

"Jez? Are you all right, love?" Mum called.

Mark nodded furiously. "Tell her you're OK, otherwise she'll be up here looking for you."

I shouted back. "I'm fine, Mum, I'm just looking for something in my room."

"Then can you come down a minute?"

Mark and I looked at each other. Who was at the door? Mark climbed up onto the bunk bed and looked out the window. "It's the police. Maybe they interrogated Tracy. She must have told them about Malcolm," Mark said.

"No, she'd never have done that. She wants to be in the gang. She would have just stood there and used sign language. And how many people can understand that? Only Malcolm – that's how clever he is."

"You'd better go," Mark said.

I stroked Malcolm's face and whispered to him, then put my finger to my lips. He had the lollipop in his cheek and the stick poking through his grinning teeth.

"You have to be quiet," I tell him.

He copies me, putting a finger to his pouting lips.

I place the other sweets in the wardrobe and he follows them.

"He'll be quiet for a bit, but watch him. Don't let him choke," I told Mark.

"What do I do if he does?"

"I don't know... try mouth-to-mouth."

Mum was whispering. The two policemen were in the doorway. I could just hear what she was saying: "We've just come back from the hospital."

I stopped halfway down the stairs and listened. The policeman looked at each other. "If he's sick, we really need to know about it. We know he's been at the Black Gate house because sniffer dogs found his trail. And there's a monkey on the loose which we think might be sick."

"Monkeys? Around here? Don't be daft," Mum said.

I was right! Malcolm must have escaped from a laboratory. Maybe they'd given him the plague or something. Being with us must have helped him. He certainly wasn't off his food.

Mum lowered her voice, like she always does,

when she tells people about me. The cops looked uncomfortable. I had to go downstairs and talk to them otherwise they might start searching the house and then they would definitely find Malcolm.

"Jez, love, these policemen need to ask you a couple of questions. Are you feeling well enough?"

I wasn't, but I nodded anyway. Anything to stop them coming inside the house. I just hoped Mark and the sweets kept Malcolm quiet for the next couple of minutes. I could see the policemen felt a bit awkward. One of them looked at me, not really at me but at my bald head – I'd forgotten to put my beanie back on.

"You were at the Black Gate, weren't you, son?"

"Yes, I just wanted to use it as a den. I didn't break anything, did I?" I said as innocently as I could.

"No, you didn't, don't worry about that. Did you see anything unusual in there?"

"No, but two men asked me the same question," I told them, because I thought if Malcolm was on the run then those other men might be after him as well. If I could get the police looking for them instead that might take their attention away from Malcolm.

"You were talking to strangers?" Mum said. "I've

told you before, Jez, don't talk to strangers in the street."

"They just asked me the same question and I told them the same answer. Which was that I didn't see anything."

"And what did these two men look like?" one of the policeman asked me with his notebook in his hand.

So I described Potato Face and Comb Head.

This seemed to interest them because they were very careful to write down everything I told them.

I couldn't resist asking: "Does the monkey have a name?"

"It's only a monkey, son. They don't have names."

Mum was looking a bit worried by this stage, and put her hand on my forehead. "I think that's enough now," she said to the policemen.

"If we could just ask a few more questions," one of them said.

I knew if they carried on they might trick me into saying something, and in that moment I felt quite grateful for having been to hospital that day.

I vomited all over the front step and their shiny black shoes.

That got rid of them.

12

There's one good thing about being sick – I mean really sick, not just pretend-stomach-ache sick so you don't have to go to school that day – and that's being fussed over the rest of the day. You can have anything you want, provided you don't get sick again, and watch DVDs all day.

And that means that Mum can usually get a day off work. Once she knew I was OK, she left me lying in front of the TV and went out to the local shops, and that gave me time to go back upstairs and see how Malcolm was. It was a crucial time and I knew we'd never get away with having Malcolm in my room for another night. We had to think of something.

"They're going to shoot Malcolm," Mark said. "Because if they've infected him already with a deadly virus then what else are they going to do? One thing is for sure – you shouldn't be anywhere near him," he insisted.

I sat down next to the wardrobe door. A crunching and slurping sound came from inside.

"There's nothing wrong with Malcolm, I'm sure of it. And even if there is it can't be infectious because none of us have come out in any spots or rashes and your flesh hasn't turned to jelly and we haven't got any blood coming out our eyes and ears."

"You had that nosebleed!" Mark said.

"I always have nosebleeds, you know that."

"I just don't see how we're going to smuggle him out the house," Mark said. We could hear sucking noises from inside the wardrobe, but the lollipops weren't going to last for ever. Mark looked out the window. "There's a cop car parked around the corner. They're watching us. They must suspect something."

"We have to ask Tracy what happened," I said.

"Well, we can't phone her because she can't use a phone, can she?" said Mark.

"She's deaf, not blind! Text her." How was he ever going to run the country if he couldn't think of that?

"I don't have her number," he said.

Neither did I. Well, you can't get everything right all the time.

"Phone Skimp and tell him to get Tracy and

meet us down at the caravan," I told him.

"How are we going to get Malcolm there?"

"I don't know yet. Can you drive Mum's car?"

"Dad showed me reverse and first gear," he said.

"That might look a bit suspicious going backwards and crawling at five miles an hour," I told him. There was a fluttering of butterflies in my chest that just would not settle. They migrated to my stomach and then came back again. I think this is what Dad might have been talking about when he said we shouldn't be scared. I was scared all right because we were very close to Malcolm being discovered.

"Always look on the bright side of life," Dad would often say. That's probably what made him a popular postie. Or he'd sing: *When you walk through a storm hold your head up high* – all of that stuff; or he'd say: "Every cloud has a silver lining"; and "You never know what's round the next corner"; and his classic line was always: "Remember these four words when you're feeling down – This Too Will Pass." He had tons of things to say about being cheerful as long as we didn't mention Michael Owen.

And then just when I couldn't keep my head up high while I was looking for a silver lining, and knowing exactly what was round the next corner – the police – Dad, as always, arrived just in the nick of time.

Because he had been up since four that morning and was working a double shift, which is called Bike Route Two, it meant he usually came home between shifts. He's supposed to go back to the sorting office, but because of 'circumstances at home' they usually let him stop off and have a cup of tea and see everything is all right. What he usually does is have an hour's sleep.

I heard his bicycle bell. And then the key in the front door. "Anybody home?" He always says that even though he knows we're there. He shouted: "What do we want? Each other! When do we want it? Now! Jez! Where're you, son?"

Mark wasn't supposed to be at home, of course, so he couldn't go downstairs. "Listen," I told him, "do as I said, get hold of Skimp. We'll get down to the caravan somehow. I've got an idea."

I went downstairs as he was giving Mum a hug.

"Hey, Jez, how are you feeling?"

He picked me up and hugged me too.

"I'm all right, I thought I might carry on with

my project because Mark is letting me use his computer again."

"What a cracking brother you have," he said, putting me down again. "You're all right though, are you?"

I nodded.

"He threw up," Mum said from the kitchen. "The police were here."

"Oh yeah? I bet they weren't selling double glazing, were they?"

"No, I don't think they have time for second jobs," I told him.

"I should hope not, with all the burglaries around here."

Mum told him everything as he tried to rescue the biscuit he had just dunked. He gave up.

"Ah, well. No harm done then. But you shouldn't go in that old place. They're quite right, it is dangerous. Don't go in there any more. Yeah?"

I nodded.

"Good lad." And he kissed my forehead. "Pity about their shoes, hey?" And he rolled his eyes, making that face.

"Right, I'm gonna grab an hour or so kip. So, if

you don't feel very well come and climb in with me. Mum has got a check-up at the dentist. Okay?"

What you need when you have a major escape plan in mind is not to have grown-ups around. They get in the way. I told Mark my idea and once he'd told me I was a lunatic, he phoned Pete-the-Feet and Rocky as well as Skimp. This will be a combined gang effort. So I waited until I saw Mum reversing down the drive and their bedroom was in darkness. Dad had closed the curtains, which meant he wouldn't see what I was going to do.

Mark and I each took one of Malcolm's hands and guided him down the stairs. He made those little chirping noises, which soon quietened when I held him. I stroked his head and whispered to him. "You mustn't be scared, I am going to look after you, but you have got to be very brave."

I felt sure that Malcolm was learning more and more English every day. He nodded his head and touched my face, then grinned. His lips came out and made that funny shape and then he kissed me. I had given him Mark's teddy bear, which he hugged. I knew one day we would find someone to love it again.

Mark came in the kitchen door. "We're ready," he said.

He'd brought Dad's bike round to the back of the house and I eased Malcolm into one of the big red bags and tucked teddy in with him. We used the straps from the pram to tie him in. I signed for him to be quiet and that I loved him. Then I zipped the bag around him and left just enough room for his nose and mouth to peep out for air.

"I'll go first," Mark said. "Are you sure you feel strong enough to do this?"

I'd given Malcolm a couple of bananas, and eaten one myself, washed down with a high energy drink. I was sure I could get as far as the industrial estate. It was Mark who had the difficult job of drawing the police away. That's called a diversionary tactic.

"I'll see you in Piccadilly," he said.

"Scott's Bar," I replied. Which is what two prisoners on the run say to each other in *The Great Escape*, a classic war film that Rocky knows back to front and which we have to watch at least once a month. I've been to London, but have no idea where Scott's Bar is – but it means that we'll escape and be reunited. That's called being hopeful.

I waited. Mark was on the street, rattling along on his skateboard. Mrs Tomkinson was already in her front garden waiting to give the bin men a piece of her mind because they always drop bits of her rubbish on the pavement. Mark did a very fancy turn, the police car was right there on the corner, and he flipped her wheelie bins open as he went past.

"Hey! You! Mark Matthews! I'll speak to your mother! You lout!"

Mark tormented her a few moments longer, doing that really annoying heel flip action, which makes the board clank every time. Grown-ups hate that noise.

One of the policemen got out the car and shouted: "All right you, clear off!"

Mark ignored him. He was very casual. He leaned his body back on his board and kicked over the kerb, slamming her lid down again. I could have stood there all day and watched him torment Mrs Tomkinson. "You flaming hooligan!" she shouted.

And the more Mrs Tomkinson shouted the more it attracted other interested parties in the street. Peacock's Feather couldn't contain herself any longer. She was yapping and barking.

"Shut that flaming dog up!" Mrs Tomkinson yelled.

By now the policeman was halfway across the street. That's when Peacock's Feather got over the gate and went for Mark. He spun around, crouched and zoomed past the policeman, who was then between Mark and the demented dog-from-hell. The policeman was, to be kind, a tad overweight. Dad always says police officers seem to be getting younger all the time. I think they're getting fatter. The policeman saw the insane dog and ran. He couldn't get into his car so he lumbered across the road and climbed over Mr Brumley's fence, almost skewering himself on the posts. His trousers definitely couldn't take the strain and there was a long rip down his leg. And then the dog cornered him. The other policemen got out the car and bravely tried to call off Peacock's Feather. She turned on him. He ran back to the car.

You can't say you don't get value for money from our local police.

Once he was back in the car, the policeman tried to drive it between the dog and the other cop. And that's when I launched Operation Free Malcolm. I pedalled out into the street and turned away from the crazy scene outside Mrs Tomkinson's. We were on our way to freedom!

I used every back alley and back street I knew. Some of them were cobbled and the bike rattled as we shuddered across them. A small face with a tea cosy on it looked out the zip bag. His teeth chattered as we went over every bump and cobble.

My eyeballs bounced up and down in their sockets. I started to feel giddy. This probably wasn't the best day in the world in which to escape. I pulled up the bike and leant against the wall and threw up again. We'd have to get onto a better road, otherwise I'd keep puking for the rest of the day and Malcolm would have no teeth left.

I was sweating and had the shakes but I had to keep going, it wasn't that far to the industrial estate. Then, as I turned the corner into Smith's Lane, I saw Mark scorching along the pavement like the Silver Surfer. I suddenly felt very proud of my older brother. As I clattered down the alley I could see he was parallel to us on the other street. I pedalled faster, keeping pace with him.

And then I heard the siren.

There was a flash of blue and yellow and a police

car overtook him. The same two policemen who had been keeping watch on us jumped out the car and cornered Mark. Exertion and fear made me breathless. I didn't know what to do. Malcolm chattered and hid behind the fingers of his hand as he cringed back into the darkness of the bag. He was probably picking up on my nervousness. I saw the cops questioning Mark. What could they be saying to him? He hadn't done anything wrong except irritate Mrs Tomkinson and the whole street does that on a daily basis.

Jet Fuel For Your Body said the label on the bottle I pulled out my pocket. I glugged the purple liquid down as fast as I could. A small hand snaked out the bag. Malcolm was thirsty. I left him a third of the bottle and passed it inside to him. Suddenly the bag was bouncing almost out of the rack. Malcolm was screeching like he'd swallowed some of Dad's home-brewed wine, which everyone thinks is wonderful for cleaning the kitchen floor. Dad thinks they like it and no one has the heart to tell him otherwise. Dad! It must have been Dad who'd set the police on us. Mrs Tomkinson and Peacock's Feather must have made such a racket that Dad would have woken up, seen that his bike was missing, that I was missing – and then he'd have gone running out the house looking for me. Then the police would have seen him. "What's wrong, postie?" (he'd have dozed in his uniform) they would have asked. "Someone's nicked your bike?" they'd have said, gobsmacked.

I suddenly realised that this could be a major criminal offence, stealing the property of the Royal Mail. Not only that, but if they zoomed off before questioning Dad properly they might think that the Royal Mail's letters and parcels had been stolen.

The bike was bouncing because Malcolm was going ballistic. I felt panic surging up like gunge from an unblocked drain. I couldn't leave him zipped up in there any longer. I wrapped my fleece around the crossbar, making a saddle for him to sit on. Then I eased him out the bag. That seemed to help in calming him down a bit and he clung to me. I held him close for a moment and I couldn't tell whose heart was beating faster, his or mine. I carefully sat him on the crossbar and secured him with the pram straps. He gripped the handlebars in the middle and rocked backwards and forwards. Then I started pedalling like crazy.

I just managed to see Mark being put into the back of the police car as I clattered away across the cobbled alleyway. I wondered how long he could hold up under questioning. Rocky always said you should be able to last at least two days under interrogation. That's what the soldiers in the Special Forces do in their training. But I don't think twelve-year-old Mark Matthews of 16 Wentworth Drive fell into that category. And if Dad was part of the interrogation team I probably had less than ten minutes before Mark cracked.

When you're scared it's good sometimes just to make a noise. Otherwise the noise gets trapped inside and can jangle your nerves and turn into a monster's claws that start climbing up inside, trying to scratch its way out of your belly button. So what you do is open your mouth wide and just shout: "Aaaaaaaaaaaaah!" Except of course when you're bumping over cobbles it comes out as: "Ag-ug-ug-ug-ug-ug-ug," as if you were gargling.

An important thing to remember is to watch out for flies.

There's a video sequence on the CCTV camera near the main road, next to the Flying Fish & Chip Shop, of a nine years, eleven months and thirteen day old boy on a bike wearing a beanie, with his mouth wide open and tears streaming from his eyes because it was so cold. On the crossbar is a monkey wearing a Steven Gerrard Number 8 red shirt and a tea cosy on his head and he's clutching the handlebars. The monkey looks terrified but in fact, as I told everyone later, he's having a wonderful time, it's me who couldn't see where I was going. I'm the one who's scared stiff. No question. Another camera just past the betting shop shows the same two wide-eyed primates whizzing past an old lady, who gets such a fright she drops her shopping.

Then, when the boy on the bike – me – swallows a fly and starts coughing and spitting, they narrowly miss a Dairy Crest delivery van, thanks to the extraordinary skill of the monkey who tries to duck out of the way of the impending crash and forces the rider – me – to swerve just in time.

The milk van shuddered to a halt on the cobbles and a dozen bottles of full-cream milk spilled onto the road. The monkey and me then swerved out of sight into Millbrook Lane, which, as everyone round here knows, is a dead end into the industrial estate.

I didn't know about the cameras until later, but when they hauled Mark away I thought that any minute there was going to be a helicopter chase. You know, like you see on those television shows where the police are in hot pursuit of joyriders travelling at high speed. Though, I wasn't sure whether a Royal Mail bicycle qualified for high speed, but the joy bit turned out to be true.

Once I realised we weren't being chased and had wiped the tears from my eyes, spat out the remains of the fly and got the bike onto a smooth surface, we scorched along. It was downhill with no traffic and I did a *Titanic* number and raised my hands off the handlebars. Malcolm did the same. I was laughing and Malcolm did his screechy thing, which told me he was having fun as well.

Down through the bottom bend, past the tile shop, around the corner from the Big Discount Carpet Warehouse and then finally, as the road narrows, a quick surge up onto the pavement past the side entrance to Scanlon's Wrought

Iron Works: Established 1987.

It's down there, under the old tin-roofed sheds, where Skimp's dad has his caravan locked up. This was where Malcolm was going to live until we could think of a way of getting down to the docks, stowing away on a container ship, and getting him back to Africa. Though we hadn't worked that part out yet and might have to settle for smuggling him into Whipsnade Animal Safari Park.

That's when I got hurt.

Just as I pedalled hard around the corner I saw Skimp and Pete-the-Feet in the distance standing next to the shed. Skimp's dad's car was there and he was waving his finger and shouting. I couldn't hear what he was saying because of the noise from the extractor fans of the iron works.

Rocky was standing next to Tracy, who was talking nineteen to the dozen with her hands. Skimp's dad made a really ugly face and yelled at her – right in her face – and she stepped back. Skimp grabbed his dad's arm, trying to protect her, but his dad gave him a clout around the head. It was obvious he had sussed out that Skimp had stolen the keys. The whole gang had been caught.

It wasn't right at that moment I got hurt, it was half a minute later. I slammed on the brakes, lay the bike at an angle, stuck my foot out, slid across the gravel, and shouted at Malcolm to hold on while I did my totally unexpected and brilliantly executed slide.

It was just after that I got hurt.

I turned the bike and pedalled like mad. Malcolm's feet gripped the crossbar, he was hanging on for dear life, bobbing up and down, chattering away. For a moment I thought he was just making a fuss about my daring escape, but it wasn't that. Two men had appeared around the corner, right in front of us – it was Potato Face and Comb Head!

They yelled at us and ran with their arms outstretched, trying to stop us getting past them.

I jigged the bike left and right, standing on the pedals, pumping my legs as fast as I could. I was sweating so much my beanie felt as though it was soaked.

And then, around the corner came the police car with Mark in the back. Potato Face and Comb Head were between us. If one lot didn't get us the others would.

There was a gap in the wire mesh fence – I went for it.

Potato Face lunged and missed, and yelped in pain because he landed in the gravel. I was too scared to laugh or call him names because I was trying to navigate through the back yard of the iron works where there's all kind of things stacked. There are gates and doors and fencing, oil drums and pallets and a sharp piece of aluminium stripping that's come away from the edge of a crate.

That's when I got hurt.

It caught my leg as I flew past. It really hurt. My jeans ripped and there was a scorching tear across my skin. I had to ignore it because Malcolm was throwing me off balance and I had to concentrate, had to keep going. Comb Head was right behind me. For someone that old with such a bad hairstyle he could run really fast.

That's called deceptive.

I could hear him grunting with effort. Malcolm was screaming. He'd looked behind us and seen Comb Head just about close enough to grab me. A forklift came out the works' shed with rolls of piping on the front. The driver saw a kid on a big red bike, and a monkey wearing a Liverpool FC shirt with his ears sticking out a tea cosy, and he slammed on his brakes.

The pipes rolled. They just missed us. But they didn't miss Comb Head.

I didn't even look back at the forklift truck driver shouting and swearing. Or at the policeman running down the yard towards them. I hunched my shoulders and ran on the pedals, making them go like crazy.

We had escaped.

But my leg hurt a lot, warm blood trickled down inside my trousers. Either that or I'd wet myself.

No. It was blood.

13

I was shivering with nerves and the cold wasn't helping. It was getting dark and we had only just managed to get out of the industrial estate. There were some abandoned warehouses right on the edge of a disused railway line, and it was so overgrown it gave us a good place to hide.

I wrapped Malcolm in my fleece and he huddled next to me while I tore the bottom of my T-shirt to wrap around my leg. It would have been easier ripping Steven Gerrard's shirt, and I'm sure he would have understood, but I just couldn't bring myself to do it. Dad had spent a lot of money on it and he promised me that one day, when I got better, he would take me into the dressing room to meet the greatest footballer in the world. It was the getting better bit that seemed to be taking a long time.

By then the blood was crusty on my leg and when I pinched the cut together it hurt more than

I'd imagined. I screwed up my face in pain. Malcolm watched me and then hid behind his open fingers. No one ever gives up in films when they get shot or injured. They just grit their teeth and carry on. Gritting teeth doesn't really do much to help the pain go away, and makes your jaw ache, but it did make me feel better. I felt like I was a soldier on the run, deep in enemy territory. Now we needed a warm place to sleep.

I checked my backpack. All I had left was a packet of crisps, a Snickers bar and an apple. Malcolm stuck his head in the bag. He came out with the packet of crisps, which he quickly tore apart. The crisps went everywhere. He was covered in them. You had to laugh – so I did. We both ate the crisps, not minding that they had been covered in dirt by Malcolm when he trampled all over them, while I sat and thought out a strategy.

It's at this point where superheroes could change into something else and escape from a situation like this, but I'm not a superhero so I had to work it out for myself. Malcolm chewed the crisps, not very elegantly I have to say, and if Mum saw him she would say: "Keep your mouth closed when you chew, Malcolm. You weren't born in a zoo." But of course in this case she'd probably be wrong.

Mum and Dad would be really worried by now, I was sure of that, but if I went home with Malcolm the police would be waiting and the RSPCA inspectors, and Malcolm would be back in the laboratory with someone hurting him.

It would have been nice to phone them so they could know I was safe. Though I wouldn't mention the cut on my leg because that kind of thing gives Mum a whole new set of worries.

I would even send them a postcard if I could, probably one of those that showed the Albert Docks, which would probably be a great idea because then they would think that I was hiding down there at the smart waterside development. But I couldn't do that either.

That's what's called being incommunicado.

So I spoke to them both in my head. "Dear Mum and Dad, I'm sorry you are worried about me, and I am sure Mum is even a bit frantic, and by now Mark will have spilled the beans and told you everything about Malcolm. As soon as I can find a way of him being safe, I'll come home. Lots of love, Beanie.

PS: It's only a scratch on my leg and nothing serious."

I thought I'd better mention the scratch.

Dad always says you never know where your thoughts can take you; well, perhaps we never know where our thoughts go. Maybe Dad would be dozing in front of the telly and my message would pop into his head.

I brushed some of the crumbs from Malcolm's fur.

"The way I see it, Malcolm, they're going to be looking out for us riding around on Dad's bike. After all, it is a bit obvious and no one would believe we're delivering letters at this time of night. So I think we should hide it here and move on to find a warm place to sleep. And, as I am a member of a democratically elected gang, I think we should have a vote on it. All those in favour?" I raised my hand and, after scraping soggy bits of crisps from under his gums with his finger and sucking it, Malcolm raised his hand.

I felt it important that he shared in the decision-making process. I wouldn't like him to think I was a tyrant. Now the crisps were finished I took his hand and we climbed under the wire fence and up across the railway embankment. There wouldn't be any trains because all the factories on this estate had closed.

Malcolm seemed very tired to me, perhaps it was because he'd had an exciting day. My leg was hurting something awful but I picked him up and carried him. I'd just realised where I was and an idea had popped into my head.

I had a plan. In my mind's eye was a picture of long motorways and yellow lights. There was a small television at the foot of my bunk and I'd lie tucked up in Dad's duvet. By morning Dad would wake me and say, "We're here."

Where was *here* going to be tomorrow?

I didn't care as long as it was far away from the people who wanted to capture Malcolm.

Suddenly the pain in my leg didn't hurt as much, even though I was carrying Malcolm. Twenty minutes later we were at the haulage yard where a dozen lorries were parked up for the night.

McKinley's Transport Company Limited.

There was a huge fence around the yard and floodlights coloured the trucks in a sickly yellow glare. They looked like prisoner-of-war-camp huts and the deep shadows between them made me think of soldiers escaping as they ran from hut to hut. On the other side of the fence from the haulage yard was a warehouse which had a refrigeration unit and down the side of the building was a big grid where the hot air came out. We stumbled, and my leg ached as if there was a hot piece of metal in it. Malcolm was also struggling. I didn't know whether it was the glare from the lights, but his eyes looked a different colour and his skin felt very hot. I knew he had a lot of fur to keep him warm – but he was shivering. I gave him the Snickers – he needed it more than me.

We crept down by the side of the warehouse and I propped him against the wall. There was plenty of rubbish that had been blown by the wind onto the mesh fence so I pulled bits of dried paper and cardboard to make us a bed over the hot air grill. It was the best I could do and it was getting really cold. I snuggled down into the paper and held him close to me, pulling my fleece over both of us like a small blanket.

I wasn't sure what to do because if he was sick like me, he might need treatment. Maybe he was infected with something? I knew being scared would make him feel worse, I always felt worse when I was scared. Maybe he'd feel better when we got a long way away from our pursuers and he stopped being frightened. He lay on my arm and made it ache, but I didn't mind because he was quiet and asleep. His face was close to mine and I smelt his bad breath, which was a bit fruity, but that's all right because he's a chimpanzee and doesn't know about dental hygiene. We'd both finally stopped shivering and lay like two monkeys clinging to each other, frightened that we might lose one another. I breathed in the pungent smell of his fur. It was wonderful.

He's semi-skimmed and I'm full cream – otherwise there's not much difference.

I'm running my socks off up and down the pitch. The floodlights cast criss-cross shadows from all the players. I see the ball spinning through the air – I take it on my chest, trap it with my foot and turn away from the tackle. I can see Steven Gerrard with his arm in the air. He's in the perfect position if I can get the ball to him. Almost in slow motion I balance myself and bring back my foot to strike the ball in a long curving loop. But I've waited too long.

There's an enormous crunch and I go down onto the grass. There's a terrible pain in my leg.

Suddenly it's all gone quiet and I turn in on myself with the pain. I can't believe it but the player who tackled me – Gobby Rogers again! – is kicking me while I'm down. That's got to be a red card. Ref! REF!

"Get up! You! Get up!" Rogers is shouting.

I jerked awake from the dream. There was a huge shadow standing over me, outlined by the yellow lamps of the haulage yard. It was a hunchback monster with wild straggly hair and a beard. I pushed back against the wall, and Malcolm screamed. Then it was the monster's turn to get a fright. It staggered back a couple of paces and fell flat on its back. It gave out a big groan and the plumes of breath coming from its jaws looked like smoke.

I'm fairly sure that anyone with superhero status would have leapt forward and throttled the monster, then thrown it over the barbed-wire-topped fence into the haulage yard.

Me, I just hugged Malcolm and let out this sort of wailing scream. Between the two of us we probably could have woken every vampire in the neighbourhood. Though of course that was a stupid thought, because everyone knows vampires are awake at night anyway.

The hunchback monster rolled on to its knees and looked at us. The light caught its face. It wasn't a monster, it was a man with a big rucksack on his back. He wore layers of clothes and a baggy raincoat. His beard was matted and stained with cigarette smoke and it looked as though he hadn't combed his hair or washed for years.

"All right, all right, shut up, will you, shut up! You'll have every security guard on the industrial estate coming to see what the racket is."

The hairy man dropped his huge rucksack, and put a finger to his lips, "Shhhh, shhhh," he said.

Malcolm copied him and put a finger to his lips. Then I stopped screaming. Malcolm and I didn't move. When we did *Oliver Twist* at school, Mr Penfold played Fagin. He was very good. He even got a standing ovation because he was so scary. So I wondered for a moment if this wasn't Mr Penfold who had tracked me down and come to scare me to death. But then the man put a finger to each nostril and blew hard, clearing his nose of snot. Mr Penfold certainly wouldn't do that, not even when he was dressed up as Fagin.

The hairy monster sat down on his rucksack and gawped at Malcom. "What in the name of all that's holy is that thing?"

I actually know lots of things that are holy. I can sometimes surprise people by telling them all that's holy. I've been to Westminster Abbey on a school tour, I did a project at school about the Vatican, I also did a photomontage of the Taj Mahal, though strictly speaking that's not really holy. And when Shazad, who's a great midfield player, by the way, did his school project on the Niujie Mosque in Beijing, we were all blown away. None of us knew there was even a mosque in China. If it was anywhere near the relocated Sweet Dreams Sweet Factory, that could be heaven.

I held Malcolm closer and thought that if he couldn't see that he was a chimpanzee wearing a tea cosy then I wasn't going to tell him.

The hairy monster sighed. "You was in my place, see? I didn't know you was a kid and I certainly didn't know you had a monkey with you. I'm sorry if I hurt you."

He was keeping his distance so I knew he wasn't going to make a grab at us. I was still ready to run if I had to, even though my leg was throbbing.

The hairy monster nodded. "I won't hurt you, lad. It looks to me as though you're a runner."

"You're wrong," I said, "I play football."

"Running away is what I mean," he said, undoing his rucksack.

I realised this could be a really tricky moment. This man who slept rough could tell the police where we were. I immediately thought of a story. We were actually part of the circus and our van had broken down when it left town and the monkey had run away and I had gone after him and now we were lost. I have to admit it didn't sound that convincing. But before I could say anything he looked at me and shook his head.

"Never mind," he said, "it's none of my business." He pulled out some cellophane-wrapped food which looked like cheese and tomato sandwiches and tossed me one. "Here, try one of these, they're only a few days past their sell-by date. I get them at the bins at the back of Sainsbury's."

I almost blurted out that that was where Mum

worked, but I managed to swallow the words. By then he had his mouth full of food, chewing away with what looked like ravioli and tomato sauce. The juices sneaked out the corner of his mouth and got soaked up by his thick beard.

I tore open the sandwich wrapper and gave half to Malcolm, who picked the sandwich apart and ate the bits separately. I just ate.

"So, here you are, looking for a warm place to sleep. Tired and hungry, cold and away from home. I bet your mum and dad are worried about you."

I bet they were too, but I had to get Malcolm away first. I almost told him that I was on a mission, but I stopped myself. Rocky once told us that when you get interrogated they always try and appear friendly to start with so that you tell them things about yourself. The best thing to do is to say as little as possible. So I kept chewing.

"How old are you, boy?"

"Nine years, eleven months and thirteen days," I said. I doubted if that was valuable information.

"That's a bit young for going on the road. I didn't run away from home until I was eighteen."

"'I'm not running away from home," I told him.

His eyes were all watery as he gazed at me. "I've got a pay-as-you-go phone. You sure you don't want to phone your mum and dad?"

It was a huge temptation. I could phone home and tell them not to worry, that I'd be back just as soon as I had found a safe place for Malcolm, wherever that might be. But then the hairy monster would have their telephone number. I bet he'd phone them back and get a reward or something for finding us.

I shook my head.

"Fair enough. So why is the monkey wearing a tea cosy? Did he use to work in a café?" He chuckled and bits of food came out of his mouth. I wasn't sure what to say because I don't think chimpanzees have worked in a café anywhere in the world.

"His head was cold," I said.

"And what about your tea cosy? Is that something your mother knitted for you?" He cleared his gums of food, just like Malcolm. There's definitely a strong link between humans and monkeys. Except monkeys mind their own business.

"It's a beanie," I told him, "Skimp's mum bought it for me at the market."

"You're a strange one," the hairy monster said.

"In all my days I've never seen such a scrawny kid running around loose with a monkey on his arm."

He tossed a carton of orange juice at our feet and I tore off its tab and guzzled. I hadn't realised I was so thirsty. Then I quickly gave it to Malcolm, who managed to spill it all over his Number 8 shirt.

"All right," said the monster, pulling the straps tight on his rucksack. "You can have my pitch tonight, but you'd best be gone tomorrow. I'm getting old and I need a warm place to kip. Y'understand, lad?"

I nodded because I wouldn't be there tomorrow. "I promise," I told him.

He hauled the rucksack onto his back. "Does the monkey have a name?"

That had to be another trick question. I remembered the policeman at the house. "Don't be daft. He's a monkey. Monkeys don't have names," I said.

"I don't see why not," he said, staggering to his feet under the weight of the rucksack, "they're not much different from us."

He knew! Here was someone who understood.

"Two per cent," I happily told him.

"Oh yeah… right… well, that's a strange name for

a monkey, but then like I said, you're a strange lad."

He wagged a finger at me. "Tomorrow. Don't forget. Be gone."

Malcolm wagged a finger back at him.

And then the hairy monster disappeared into the shadows. It just goes to show, you can't judge people by how they look. There he was, looking quite terrifying but he'd given us something to eat and drink and his bed for the night. Mum always says we should never talk to strangers, that they might be serial killers. Every stranger is a serial killer as far as Mum is concerned.

There was no time left to think of what else might come out of the night. Some of the big lorries were starting up. Diesel fumes blew from their exhausts, blue puffs like dragon's breath.

The long haul drivers were heading out.

Once I was sure the hairy monster stranger had gone, I lifted Malcolm and headed for the corner of the fence.

14

Old Barry wasn't really that old, but I remember Dad telling me he was fairly useless as a security guard on the main gate at McKinley's. He hated the cold and would sit hunched up in his tiny gate house with a small telly, flask and sandwiches.

A couple of the early-start drivers were getting ready to leave, and Old Barry was opening the gates. That was good for us, because it meant he was at the far end of the yard and wouldn't have a chance of seeing me and Malcolm climb under the mesh fence in the corner – even if he *wasn't* fairly useless.

One of the drivers had already started up his lorry, probably to get the cab's heater going. He walked around its trailer checking that all the lights and everything were working, that the tyres looked all right and that the big doors at the back were still security sealed with their little tag.

And that was when I climbed up into the cab

on the opposite side with Malcolm. For a horrible moment I nearly panicked, because I'd forgotten about the extremely comfortable air-assisted seats – the most comfy you can get. They hiss when you sit on them! It seemed so loud I was sure the driver would run back, thinking one of the tyres had gone down. But he didn't. I think being so scared made the noise seem louder than it actually was. Being scared can do that.

I pulled Malcolm up into the bunk behind the driver's seat and tugged the half-curtain closed. This is where drivers keep all their stuff, and they always have the curtain closed for security so no one can look inside the cab and see if there's anything worth nicking. There was a duvet, pillows, a small telly and a couple of books. I pushed Malcolm up into the overhead bunk.

The driver would only be allowed to be behind the wheel for a few hours and then he'd stop and probably go and have a cup of tea in a motorway café. Until then we should be okay – provided Malcolm stayed quiet.

I tucked him in behind me and nuzzled his face, stroking it, signing for him to be quiet. He watched me.

DAVID GILMAN

Trusting me. Then he hid behind his hand again. The driver climbed back in the cab and slammed the door. The big engine started up, rumbling, waiting for him to engage the clutch and push the gear stick into first. The lorry creaked forward.

"All right then, Barry, see you on Wednesday!" he called to the fairly useless security guard.

Then the air brakes hissed and the lorry rolled into the street. I could hear the indicator light clicking then felt the heavy sway of the lorry as it swung around the corner.

I peeped through the curtain and saw the back of the man's head. The dashboard lights glowed warmly and in the distance I could see our road to freedom. The motorway.

Then as we pulled out of the haulage yard I glimpsed a blue light flashing. They had tracked us! Maybe they used dogs to follow our scent. How did they find us so quickly? Two policemen climbed out of their car near the place where the hairy monster found us. The lorry swung away, but I could see in the big wing mirrors a figure come out of the darkness and point down the side of the building where we had been.

The kind-hearted hairy monster had turned us in and we had escaped just in time. So much for trusting people no matter how they look. But they couldn't catch us now. The driver moved up a couple of gears and the cops soon disappeared from the wing mirrors.

The heater blew warm air into the cab, the driver pressed a button and classical music came out of the speakers. It was very slow and gentle, like a lullaby. I made sure I was wedged in when I snuggled down and felt Malcolm put his arm around me. This was the safest place we could be and the lorry's gentle movement began to rock me asleep.

But as I closed my eyes I was thinking of those policemen. How long would it be before they told Dad we'd been sighted? The first thing he'd say would be: "Where? McKinley's? That's where I used to work."

Time was running out. My leg hurt and I felt sick. I couldn't let myself fall asleep. I had to stay awake long enough to think of another plan. When kids went missing the police did everything they could as quickly as they could – and when a child went missing with a monkey that had escaped from

research laboratory they probably moved twice
as quick.

What to do?

Think, Beanie, think!

I watched the dashboard's digital clock. The seconds
and minutes just kept disappearing into some kind
of electronic cyber hole. Time just wouldn't slow
down and give me a chance to work things out. It
had been two hours since we drove out the yard and
now it was three in the morning. I had never been
up this late, not even when we went on the Channel
ferry to Disneyland in France.

I just wanted to rest and cuddle up to Malcolm.
He lay there watching me. He couldn't sleep either.
Did he have a memory? Could he remember what
they did to him? I touched his face. Then I clenched
my fist and moved it in a circle on my chest. *I'm sorry.*

He pointed at me, then put one hand in the other
and tugged. That meant I was his friend. He wrapped
his arms around me. I could feel him trembling.
I had an almost uncontrollable urge to reach through
the curtain and tap the driver on his shoulder.
I would tell him everything and he'd feel so sorry for

Malcolm that he would drive us exactly where we needed to go. Which was where? To tell the truth, I had given up the idea of getting to Africa. Getting this far had had been difficult enough. I would have to find an animal sanctuary and maybe the driver knew where one might be.

But of course I didn't tap him on his shoulder. That would have been incredibly irresponsible. He would have got such a fright that he might crash the lorry and then we would be in an even bigger mess.

The driver shifted gears, and when I peeped back through the curtain I saw that we were heading up a slip road for a motorway service station. Mist settled across the dark trees and the motorway lights were smothered and dull. The driver took the exit that said 'lorries' and slowed right down, then carefully, just like Dad used to do, eased into a space. We were surrounded by blacked-out lorries, huddling in the darkness, like Malcolm and me.

When the driver switched off the engine and his lights, he climbed down and headed through the narrow channel between the parked lorries towards the motorway café's fuzzy lights and then disappeared from view.

I eased Malcolm out the bunk, got him onto my back and climbed down. The air-assisted seat sighed. It was cold outside the cab and the smell of diesel stung my throat. If anyone had figured out that we might have been in one of the lorries leaving McKinley's then we needed to find another way of escape. A change of vehicle, that's what they did in the movies.

Limping, I edged along the gaps between the lorries. Most of them had curtains drawn across the windscreen and side windows, as drivers slept in their cabs. I was struggling with my leg and Malcolm's weight. Sweat made my beanie feel like a wet cat on my head – all soggy and scratchy.

I was worried about Malcolm, he didn't seem to be that well and I was sure he needed more food. Trouble was, I only had thirty-three p in my pocket. I was keeping the apple we had left for a real emergency. I took Malcolm into the trees and untied the piece of T-shirt from my leg. The bleeding had stopped but it looked red and puffy. Anyway, the strip was enough to wrap around a thin tree and tie onto Malcolm's harness that he still wore.

He looked a bit alarmed so I spoke to him quietly.

There was just us and the weird lights in the fog, so no one would see him if he stayed quiet. Even if he squeaked a bit it should be all right because of the whooshing sound of the motorway traffic in the background.

"You stay here," I said, but used my hands as well. "I'm going to get you some food and a paracetamol." Though I didn't know how to say paracetamol in sign language.

I zipped him up in my fleece, and when I looked back the mist and shadows had camouflaged him completely. I felt a horrible tug inside my stomach. It was as if I was abandoning him – and he didn't know that I was coming back. He was just a small chimpanzee all on his own, tied to a tree in the fog at a motorway service station. How brave was that?

I ran.

The girl at the till had a stud in her nose, and another one in her tongue. I didn't think she was really interested in serving anyone at that time of the morning. She clicked her tongue and the metal stud tapped against her teeth. For a second I thought of Tracy and wished she was here so she could talk more to Malcolm. I'm sure she'd be able to make him understand a lot more than I could. Tracy only had one stud, though, and this girl looked as though Dad had been at her with his DIY staple gun.

I was trying not to panic.

The girl looked at me. "I'm not allowed to sell you medicine at your age."

She was suspicious! If I opened my mouth too wide my heart would have jumped out and lain wobbling on the checkout counter. I smiled. That kept it below throat level.

"Oh, they're not for me. They're for my dad. He just came in and got those bars of chocolate for me. There he is, the man in a leather jacket carrying his take-away coffee," I wheezed. It was either nerves or the damp.

She bent forward and looked towards the exit of the café area, where the man was going out towards the cars.

I couldn't get the voice in my head to shut up: Don't panic! Be natural. Play it cool. That's called being nonchalant.

"I said I wanted a banana and he said that while I was here I should get him some paracetamol for his headache. Because he'd forgotten to buy some."

She looked at me as if to say, "Oh, yeah?"

I smiled.

She didn't. She clicked. And held up my banana. "Only one?"

"I'm not that hungry," I said.

She sighed, holding out her hand for my money. "You're short," she said.

"I know, but my dad says I'll grow taller when I get older."

She stared at me like a zombie. The dark rings under her eyes weren't make-up.

"Whatever," she said and took the banana back. "Thirty-four p for the banana, thirty-two p for the paracetamol." She gave me one p change.

I looked at her, uncertain whether to plead for the banana.

"What?" she grunted. "You said you weren't that hungry. You can't have both."

There's not a lot you can do with one p, so I put it in the Flying Ambulance collection box. You never know when you might need them and it does no harm to have made a donation.

And if she ever goes out in a lightning storm

with all those studs, she might be thankful as well.

My hands were shaking something terrible. I got a plastic water bottle from a dustbin and headed to the toilet to find a tap. Providing I didn't put my lips on the rim of the water bottle, I didn't think I would catch the plague or anything. Though the way I was feeling, I might have had it already – what if Sweet Dreams Sweet Factory really had been a biological warfare site? What if Mum had lied? Maybe that's how I got sick in the first place! My mind wandered as I filled the bottle in the toilet's tap below a sign that told me it was drinking water.

Back outside I got a fright. The yellow lights soaked into the fog like kitchen towel soaks up spilled orangeade. It looked horrible, like the whole world was sick. The mist swirled and shapes changed. I couldn't find him.

"Malcolm?"

I heard a small cry. He sounded frightened.

"Malcolm, I'm here, I'm here… where are you…?" I had to push through the mustard cloud. Then suddenly I saw his face peering out beneath the tea cosy. Droplets clung to his fur and the fleece, he looked like a sugar-coated doormat.

As soon as I reached him he clung to me and we held each other. It was like he was asking me never to leave him again and I was promising I wouldn't.

It said on the packet of paracetamol that if you're under twelve you should only take half a tablet. I didn't know how old Malcolm was and I was worried that if I gave him the wrong dose I might hurt him. But he was definitely not well. I didn't even know if chimpanzees could have paracetamol. But then I remembered Peacock's Feather. She always got a really bad allergy every spring. Her nose used to run, her eyes would close, she'd get lumps all over the place. The vet was going to charge Mr Peacock more than he paid for his Sky subscription to give her injections so he went down to Superdrug and got a packet of antihistamine off the shelf, and fed her those. She was soon back to being a total lunatic.

I gave Malcolm two tablets. If he had survived one of Mum's Valium, these shouldn't hurt him.

He was wheezing and I didn't know if it was due to the fog. I untied him just as a lorry's headlights caught us. For a second I froze. Then they dimmed, the engine stopped but the sidelights were still on.

A shadow jumped down and ran into the fog behind the trailer. I only hesitated for a second because I realised the lorry driver had pulled in and ducked behind his trailer for a quick pee.

"Come on, Malcolm, that's our new ride," I told him, grabbing his hand and walking as quickly as I could to the lorry. If the driver had only stopped for a quick pee we didn't have much time. I climbed up on the passenger side and opened the door. It was a Renault Magnum, considered by some to be a top-spec vehicle – the King of the Road, that's what Dad always called them – though I didn't have time to explain that to Malcolm.

The cab smelled warm and stale, like my bed at home when I read under the duvet with my torch. I pulled Malcolm up into the bunk behind the curtain that was already closed. There were a couple of fluffy toys on the dashboard and pictures of a pretty girl with big eyes and an even bigger smile. One of them was stuck on a piece of card, and in different coloured crayon it said *Daddy's girl.*

It was quiet in there, like a secret place where no one can find you. The door opened and the driver thumped into the seat, slammed the door and made a shivery noise because it was cold outside. The engine started, the lights stared into the fog.

We were on our way again.

Once we got onto the motorway it seemed that the fog was lifting, but we were going slowly, the big engine droned on and on as the driver kept it in low gear. It was going to be ages before we got anywhere.

The driver leaned forward in his seat, gazing into nothingness, searching for tail lights. I remembered Dad doing that – watching for anyone in trouble who'd stopped in the fog.

Malcolm was quiet, his eyes only half open. He held the palm of one hand flat and then tapped it with the other. I nodded and made the same movement with mine. *I'm happy too,* I told him in my head.

He put his hand in mine and closed his eyes. I was burning hot now. Maybe it was the warm cab. My head banged onto my chest, I struggled to keep my eyes open. I couldn't stay awake. Maybe I didn't have to. The fog was our invisible shield. No one would ever find us now.

The clock on the dashboard said 03.58.

We were safe.

I closed my eyes.

It felt like I was asleep for hours. Maybe even days. You can't imagine how complicated all my dreams were. I was exhausted when I woke up.

There was a sudden hiss.

Then silence.

I peeped through the curtain. The clock said 04.03. I'd only been asleep for five minutes! Malcolm was still asleep, wheezing like the wind through the eaves of the Black Gate.

The hissing was the air brakes. The lorry had stopped and the driver had gone, swallowed up by a blue swirling cloud outside. I was still groggy and I couldn't believe there was an ice-cream van parked in front, and that the driver had got out for something like a double whippy chocolate flake. Which, in this freezing fog at four o'clock in the morning, was a serious ice-cream addiction.

It wasn't an ice-cream van.

The police car and ambulance had blocked us in. Policemen wearing yellow striped jackets came towards us – and there was another man with a big net, big enough to catch a whale in. I must have still been dreaming. Mum and Dad got out of the police car, but one of the policemen extended his arms and held them back. Anyone would think this was a dangerous situation.

I think it was, for Malcolm.

I shook him gently – we could still make a run for it. "Malcolm, we've got to go. Wake up." He barely moved when he looked at me, and then he pulled the little fingers on each hand down across his chest. I tried to remember stuff that Tracy had told me. "I don't know what you're saying," I whispered. I could feel tears sting my eyes. "I don't…" I told him again.

How can you love someone so much and not understand what they are trying to tell you? Then I remembered. He was telling me he was sick. My friend was really sick and I couldn't help him any more.

I was trying to get my brain to work, but my head was on fire and the cut on my leg was thumping faster than my heart. This was it – no Piccadilly, no Scott's Bar, no Great Escape.

The door opened a crack and a policeman put his head into the cab. He was dripping wet and the freezing air suddenly filled the cab. He smiled. "You're Jez, aren't you? It's all right, son, we're not going to hurt your mate, but he's sick and we have to get him to hospital."

Drizzle distorted the windscreen. There was a weird-shaped man holding the net.

"No! You're going to do experiments on him!" I shouted.

He hadn't moved, or made a grab for Malcolm.

On the end of the policeman's nose there was a drip of rain, which he wiped away. "I promise we won't do anything like that. He'll be all right… hang on a second."

He closed the door and I saw him walk towards Mum and Dad, who were huddling from the drizzling fog, and he also called out to someone else, waving his arm to another policeman – there must have been dozens of them surrounding us but I could only see three or four.

They brought out two men from another police car. The policeman said something to Dad, who nodded, and then came towards the cab.

I was shivering. Shaking from head to toe. There was no way I could escape with Malcolm now. The cab door opened and Dad stuck his head inside. He didn't try to grab me or anything. I pulled

Malcolm closer to me. If I held on to him they would have to drag us out together.

Dad rolled his eyes. Just like when he saved me from the top of Sweet Dreams Sweet Factory. "All right, Jez?"

I nodded, but I think I was doing that anyway because of the shakes.

Dad turned the ignition key and flipped on the headlights and the wipers. The blades swished away the rain.

"See those two ugly blokes?" he said.

I stared through the windscreen and saw the policemen standing with men in handcuffs. It was Potato Face and Comb Head!

"They stole Malcolm and thanks to you the police have caught them. But Malcolm is sick, son. He really is. You have to let them help him."

It was very quiet. Just Malcolm's breathing and my teeth chattering. It was so hot in there.

Dad reached in and lifted me from the bunk. He didn't even pull a face or anything with the effort, he's so strong he could probably have done it with one hand. Then it was freezing cold and the drizzle tickled my face. Dad held me close to him, just like I carried Malcolm. It was all a bit swirly. The motorway traffic was going past, the police had flickering warning torches, the ambulance had a bar of blue and white light dish-dashing backwards and forwards. Mum said something that I couldn't hear. Maybe all the fog had got into my ears. Then a man in a green jacket with a yellow stripe across it put a survival blanket around me. It was like being a chicken wrapped in silver foil ready for the oven. But I wasn't free-range any more.

The policeman smiled, tugging the blanket a bit more over my head.

"Those men won't be stealing any more animals, Jez. We've been after them for a long time. Once we knew you'd been hiding where your dad used to work we put two and two together and checked all the CCTV cameras on the motorway service stations. We saw you climb into the cab. Now, you just relax with your mum and dad. Everything will be all right."

Dad turned so I could see the lorry. A policeman and another man – I bet it was the RSPCA inspector – lifted Malcolm down from the cab and wrapped him up as well. Dad was about to step up into the back of the ambulance, Mum was already inside. Malcolm was being put in the white van right next to me – RSPCA Animal Rescue. I wanted to tell them he's not an animal. He's nearly one of us.

Malcolm looked at me. His long bony fingers made a sign.

"I love you too," I told him.

Everything went fuzzier. The fog must have been getting thicker. Car doors slammed, the white van disappeared, a police car started up. I heard crackling voices over a radio. The ambulance driver said something into his handset. The police car led us out onto the motorway, its flashing light like a propeller churning it along.

Dad still held me so I could see through into the ambulance's cab. In front of us red tail lights shifted to one side as a siren made everyone get out of the way.

Someone must have needed help.

15

Sometimes I'm amazed at how easy it is to wake up. One minute you're in dreamland, the next you wake up into another sort of dream. It's like there's someone tugging you back. I lay still and let the bedclothes snuggle around me. Mum and Dad were there. Mum had puffy red eyes from crying and it looked as though Dad hadn't shaved for a couple of days. And he shaves every day, so something must have kept him busy.

I had to tell Dad something. I knew I would hurt his feelings, because I'd heard him say things to Mum when he thought I couldn't hear him. He was always talking about the way things were before.

Before.

I thought he might be living in the past. And you know there are some things you just can't change. Things happen, you don't want them to, but they do. And they're not always nice things either.

"Dad," I said.

He held my hand. "Yes, Jez?"

My voice sounded like a whisper. "I've been thinking about something really important."

He looked at me. I didn't know if I had the heart to tell him.

"What's that, son?"

I curled my finger and he put his face close to mine so only he would hear. "Now that Michael Owen has retired I don't think he's ever going to come back and play for us again," I said.

His face crumpled a bit. I think he was being very brave. There were tears in his eyes, but then he smiled. And kissed me.

"I think you're right," he said.

A doctor and nurse were muttering near the door. Mum came over and brushed her hand across my face. "You gave us all a bit of a fright," she said quietly.

Me? I don't think Mum knows what fright is. Try being chased by ugly men with bad haircuts, try talking to hairy monsters in the night, try saving...

"Where's Malcolm?"

"He's safe," Mum said.

The door opened and the nurse brought in the gang. Mark and Pete-the-Feet, Skimp and Rocky and Tracy. That was nice. I was pleased they'd let her stay in the gang. I bet it took an Emergency Meeting of the Executive Council. And someone must have voted on my behalf.

That's called voting by proxy.

The nice thing was, they were all wearing beanies. Then they took them off. Incredible! They'd all had their heads shaved. They were bald just like me.

"We had a meeting…" Mark said.

I knew I was right.

"And we've decided to call ourselves the Beanie Gang."

"That's brilliant. Even Tracy," I said.

She still spoke funny but we could all understand her. "Deaf and bald," she said, "tha' should give the bullies something to laugh about!"

Mark sat on the edge of the bed. "I have to do all the chores, so hurry up and get better, yeah?"

"I'm doing my best," I told him.

"Well, don't hang about. Mum and Dad have got a present for you. Just don't tell them you already know. Act surprised."

"What? A new bike?"

"Don't be stupid, that's your Christmas present. Oh, I wasn't supposed to tell you that."

"All right, you lot, that's enough. We don't want to tire the patient, do we?" the nurse said.

Mark and the others all signed. I laughed. They'd just said something really rude.

"Tracy's teaching us. It's our new secret code," Rocky said.

How cool is that?

Everyone was smiling. They must have been happy.

As the nurse pushed the gang out the door, Dad brought in a lady who looked quite old, like Mum, and who had the same sort of kind face. She was carrying Malcolm. And he still wore the football shirt. I think it'd been washed and ironed though.

"Malcolm!"

She put him down on the bed.

"Jez, this is Mrs Carter. She's Malcolm's owner," Mum said.

I barely heard what she was saying. Malcolm was sitting on my chest. I could barely breathe I was so happy. He was making those *whoo whoo* sounds, and touching my face.

"I run an animal sanctuary. This little chimp fell sick and those two awful men stole him from the infirmary. Malcolm, as we now call him, escaped from their van and must have hid in the Black Gate," said Mrs Carter.

"Which is where I found him."

"Thank heavens you did. Malcolm was taught to sign because he's part of a research programme in animal communication. He's actually a very clever chimpanzee."

"No one will ever hurt him for experiments?"

"Never ever. I promise. He's one of the lucky ones. And you can visit him whenever you want."

Malcolm was pinching my grapes. He pushed one into my mouth.

His hands moved. *Does it hurt?* he asked me. No. Not any more.

The End

Author's note

This story was always going to be about a young boy's view of his world, with a glance in the direction of his parents who patiently bore their distress for their sick son. Beanie saw their concern as something that went beyond his own illness as he carried on with his day-to-day life. It was his character's quirky look at the world that always held such an appeal for me and it was never going to be a story that became maudlin or morbid. It's often a stroke of luck when a writer finds such an endearing character as Beanie – doubly so when he gets to explore his own feelings with someone like Malcolm.

I had help during my research for this book – thanks go to Matthew Jones, for explaining the workings of the lorries used in the story. Thanks also to both the senior paediatrician at Derriford Hospital in Plymouth, Devon, as well as the

Derriford Children's Cancer Trust, who advised on the symptoms and treatment for young people who fall ill with leukaemia.

The survival rate for so many young people with leukaemia has increased and cancer research has become the main weapon in the on-going battle against this illness.

Cancer charities, such as *Cancer Research UK* and, in particular, the *CLIC Sargent for Children with Cancer* always need support. Many years ago when my family were struggling financially and my sister fell ill, *Sargent* made sure she had a couple of pounds a week to spend on a few personal items. It made such a difference to her. When Cancer and Leukaemia in Childhood merged with *Sargent* in 2005, their ability to help children and teenagers became even stronger.

Like Malcolm, we all need rescuing at times and, as Beanie reached out for his new-found friend, I don't think it's beyond any of us to do something similar.

David Gilman